... A Chinese laundry ticket that mytseriously turned up in a North Vietnam prisoner-of-war camp

... A whistle used in training dogs to obey commands

... A frigid girl who suddenly became an insatiable nymphomaniac

... A seemingly harmless cup of tea

These were the clues. They hid the identity of the man who held mankind's most destructive weapon in his hand.

Nick Carter had only 72 hours to find him.

NICK CARTER IS IT!

"Nick Carter out-Bonds James Bond."

—*Buffalo Evening News*

"Nick Carter is America's # 1 espionage agent."

—*Variety*

"Nick Carter is razor-sharp suspense."

—*King Features*

"Nick Carter is extraordinarily big."

—*Bestsellers*

"Nick Carter has attracted an army of addicted readers ... the books are fast, have plenty of action and just the right degree of sex ... Nick Carter is the American James Bond, suave, sophisticated, a killer with both the ladies and the enemy."

—*The New York Times*

FROM THE NICK CARTER KILLMASTER SERIES

Dedicated to the men of the
Secret Services of the
United States of America

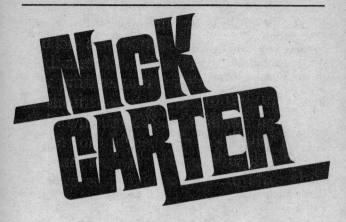

NICK CARTER

THE MIND KILLERS

CHARTER
NEW YORK

AWARD BOOKS ARE PUBLISHED BY
UNIVERSAL-AWARD HOUSE, INC.
DISTRIBUTED BY ACE BOOKS
A DIVISION OF CHARTER COMMUNICATIONS INC.
A GROSSET & DUNLAP COMPANY

I

I wondered what they were thinking about, each of them, the grim-faced, hard-jawed men, ready, waiting, eager to drop through the air to possible death. Were they thinking back, perhaps, to family, wife, mother, girlfriend? Or was the past far from their minds? Was I the only one wondering why the hell I was here?

We were moving in fast, flying high, the old C-47s bulging with men—silent, composed, alert, battle-hardened veterans. As a kind of special passenger, I was sitting just back of the pilot's cabin with Major Paul Dreiser, commander of the operation. The total force consisted of three old C-47s packed with paratroops, the specially trained, airborne commandos, and me, Nick Carter, AXE agent N3.

I had faced death many times in many ways but this wasn't my cup of tea. I was all geared to "hook up" with the rest of them, but I was damned glad they were coming along. It was a very, very special bit, this expedition, and my mind went back to the events which had brought me into it. I saw the headline again, that big, black newspaper headline which capsuled the whole strange business in a few words:

SENATOR HERBERT ATKINS AND PARTY DISAPPEAR ON FACT-FINDING TRIP.

The column below had been brief but gave all the information I needed to know.

"Senator Herbert Atkins, head of the important Foreign Relations Committee, accompanied by his young aide, Ferris Dickson, and

Miss Judy Howell, correspondent for *Tomorrow* magazine, have vanished in their special jet carrying them from South Vietnam to Formosa. The jet was piloted by Air Force Lieutenant Robert Cryder. A massive sea-air search . . . etc."

It had been a Sunday morning, a lazy Sunday morning after an active weekend. Linda had brought the newspaper in from the hall outside her bedroom, tossing it on the bed as I stretched.

I had a funny feeling about that headline the moment I read it, a premonition of more to come in that damned, unnerving way I have. I knew, then and there, I would somehow be involved. Linda noticed my frown, the long silence as I stared at the headline story.

"What is it, Nick?" she said, settling down beside me, wearing only the tops of her pajamas, her long slim legs tucked up under her. Linda Smythe had a horsewoman's figure, perhaps a little too thin but with a tensed-wire strength to it. I dismissed the Atkins story, pushing it to the back of my mind—where I knew damned well it wouldn't stay for long. But I didn't want anything to intrude on what was left of the long weekend. It had been a great weekend and Linda had been only part of it. Her place in Fairfax County, Virginia, just outside Washington, inherited from a wealthy grandmother, was made for just what we'd been doing since Friday—relaxing, riding, leisurely enjoying life. Linda's weekend riding parties and hunts were famous in the Washington social set. She invited only those people who thoroughly enjoyed horses and good living, people who appreciated and savored life, who fitted into her pattern of beautiful horses and beautiful women, good liquor and good conversation. Linda's house was more than big enough for the dozen or so guests to lose themselves at the end of the day, and I lost myself in Linda's room every night.

When I didn't answer her question, she pushed the newspaper onto the floor, aware that it had sounded a sudden, jarring note.

"I think we should forget about the morning paper," she commented crisply. She slipped off the pajama top, arching her shoulders and stretching, knowing how that pulled up her lovely, soft breasts, unusually peaked and shaped for a girl as slender as she was. Linda had the wonderful quality of enjoying her body without being in the least bit narcissistic about it. Like the thoroughbred riding horses she raised, she reveled in being what she was, young and sleek and made to be stroked.

She had enough money to buy almost anything she wanted badly enough. She had even tried to buy me once, waving all that she had and all that she was under my nose. I convinced her I was terribly interested in what she was and not at all in what she had. It had been a new experience for her, and it had increased her liking for me.

"I can be relaxed with you, Nick," she once said. "You're not out for anything but me, the girl."

That was true and also more than enough. Linda wasn't the most gorgeous thing I'd ever been with, though she was certainly an attractive girl. But she brought an open, frank, unabashed willingness to everything she did, in or out of bed. That Sunday morning, she leaned up against my chest, her breasts flattening softly, warmly against my skin. I moved and cupped a breast, my finger slowly circling the large brownish nipple.

"Oh God, Nick," she breathed. "I'm going to miss these weekends with you when you're off somewhere on one of your secret trips."

Her arms circled my neck and the nipple I touched grew firm with desire. Her legs, those long, slim, strong legs, opened to clasp my body. I knew I'd miss these weekends too; there was no question about that. I turned my head as she muzzled her face against my neck and found myself looking down at the newspaper on the floor. She raised her head and saw me staring.

"Forget that damned paper," she

demanded, and proceeded to make me do just that.

In the three weeks that followed, I almost forgot the small ticking in the corner of my mind. The newspapers had forgotten the story too, except for an occasional short, buried line. I was taking part in one of Hawk's annual refresher seminars. In between assignments, one doesn't just sit around AXE headquarters and relax.

The Chief runs a taut ship. His schedule had me at one session or another every day. They ran from special conferences on international hotspots to language refresher sessions, from physical drills to general seminars on the counterespionage activities of every major power.

I didn't mind, really. I don't usually get time to brush up on the various aspects of my special business, and there are always new things to learn. The "memory briefings," where we went through AXE files of the more unsavory characters on the international scene, were worth the price of admission alone. Some of them brought back harsh memories, some raised grim smiles and some were reminders of scores I had yet to settle.

And so I'd almost forgotten about that newspaper headline when Hawk called me into his office early on a Tuesday morning. His steel gray eyes gave me one of those grim glances which mean he's been wrestling with something he doesn't particularly understand. By the nature of our work, we are always dealing in unknowns, in unsolved puzzles and incomplete pictures. But Hawk likes to know that whatever few facts he might have are sound. If the material on hand is uncertain, he is always on edge. He was that way that morning.

"Of course you remember the disappearance of Senator Atkins and his party, N3," he began. Instantly, the little corner of my mind began to tick loudly.

"We've been given information that he and his party are alive," Hawk continued. "It came to us through usual sources, and it's been handled as top-secret, very top-secret. Word is that the senator's plane was forced down in North Vietnam, where he's being held by a band of irregulars and Vietcong, a splinter group dissatisfied with the way things have gone. They're holding him for ransom to anyone—including their own officials. Word has reached us that the senator could be rescued by a lightning military stroke. Military has prepared such a stroke under the code name Operation Senator. Of course you know what it would mean if such an operation failed, or if it got out that we were engaging in it."

"It would bring on a lot of nasty repercussions in a lot of places, I'm sure," I said. "But where does AXE fit in? It sounds like a job for the military only."

"The President himself wants us in," Hawk said. "First, the original information came to us through our sources. Second, if anything goes wrong, he wants one of our people on hand, should it be necessary for us to contact those sources. And third, there may be certain intelligence aspects to this whole thing that would require the experience our people have."

The little corner of my mind had stopped ticking. It was buzzing loudly now. "And I got the brass ring," I ventured.

"Right." Hawk smiled politely. His parting words that day were: "It's really a simple bit, N3. You're only going in with the military to stand by and question the senator later for our own report."

I found out later that on this mission "going in with the military" meant being parachuted in as part of the operation, a little item Hawk had neglected to mention. I'd been shot at in a lot of places in a lot of ways, but being a target in midair was just not my idea of "standing by." But here I was, approaching the North Vietnamese coast north of Cam Pha, the dawn sky just starting to cast gray light over the emerging shore.

Our informant had been very precise as to the location of the village where the senator and his friends were being held, the approximate number of guerrillas and renegade regulars there and the most convenient landing areas nearby. The plan was that, after the drop, the C-47s would land on a long strip of firm coastal sand and wait for our return, presumably with the senator and his party. I didn't know then—I couldn't know—that in the past three weeks a number of meetings had taken place at the exact spot we were approaching. They were meetings in which a number of most interesting terms had been freely used —terms such as "subliminal implementation," "programmed responses," "computerized mental circuits" and "advanced post-hypnosis." No, I was to find out about that later, after too much blood, and too much tragedy. All I knew at the beginning was that I was taking part in a postage-stamp-size invasion—and I wished that my premonitions didn't come so true so damned often.

Major Dreiser pointed out the window, and I saw the shoreline below, dense foliage set back, growing more distinguishable as we lost altitude. I saw the paratroopers begin to stand,

forming a curved line leading from the
door of the cabin. We were coming
down fast; the plane I rode would be
the first over the target area. As we
banked, I could see a village just back
from the shore, a small collection of
wood and leaf huts.

"Better get in line, Mr. Carter,"
Major Dreiser said. "We'll be jumping
in moments."

"I can't wait," I said, getting to my
feet. Not being Regular Army I was
wearing a nonregulation jump suit.
The door of the cabin was pulled open
and a rush of air blew in. I watched
the first man step out, then the second.
The line moved quickly. The man
before me threw me a quick grin as he
jumped, and then it was my turn. I
leaped, the M-16 in my hands, feeling
myself falling lazily through the air.
There was an almost serene quality to
my seemingly slow, tumbling motion,
though I was actually falling rapidly,
and then, there was a sharp snap as
the chute was opened automatically
by the "static lines" fastened to a
cable inside the plane.

I was falling slowly now, borne on soft air by the billowing chute. I glanced around to see the air full of figures floating under voluminous white umbrellas. The sound of rifle fire began to puncture the quiet, and I saw the ground coming up surprisingly fast. I recalled the instructions I'd been given: Bend the knees when you hit, fall flat to the ground, unhook the chute and start firing.

I felt the pull of the chute as my feet touched the ground and I was yanked backwards. I fell to the grass and almost dropped the M-16. I unsnapped the harness and ducked as the landing area erupted in furious shooting. Vietnamese raced out of the huts, firing as they came. The ground was alive with collapsed parachutes and racing paratroopers. The paratroopers set up a withering fire as they moved toward the village from three positions, a cross fire that mowed down the Vietcong guerrillas like sheaves of wheat.

I joined in the steady advance on the huts. Reaching the edge of the village, the paratroopers spread out and began small-unit approaches, racing in between and around and sometimes under the huts. I glimpsed Major Dreiser leading a group of six paratroopers in through the back of one bamboo hut, and I saw it shake from the impact of high-powered M-16 slugs.

Three Vietcong spied me and came on in short, erratic advances, firing as they came. I dropped low and let go a burst from the M-16. They staggered and dropped, twitching in a last spasm. The North Vietnamese were pouring a withering fire from inside the huts, but their aim was lousy. The paratroopers raced through the defensive fire and burst into the first line of huts with ease, silencing the defenders in each one in minutes.

I raced for the corner of a somewhat more solid building of pine with a bamboo roof. I would have made it easily except for a ten-foot mud patch right at the corner. My feet went out from under me, and I skidded into the corner post of a porch in front of the building. I tried to turn aside, but without footing it was impossible. I managed to avoid bashing my brains out on the post by raising the M-16 before my face as I crashed.

The rifle took the full impact of the collision as the edge of the post struck it dead center. I heard something snap inside the gun as I bounced backwards and landed in the mud. I looked up at three Vietcong on the porch, one with a bayoneted rifle aimed directly at me, the other two holding machetes. I rolled over in the mud, hearing the shot explode. Somehow, it missed me, and I tried to get off a burst with the M-16, but it jammed.

One of the machete-armed Vietcong leaped down at me from the porch and this time the mud got my vote of thanks as his feet slid out from under him. I leaped forward, crashing a right to his face before he could regain his feet. He went sliding backwards into the corner post and lay still.

The Vietcong with the rifle fired again, and once again the shot missed me. The rifleman swung himself over the porch and dropped to the ground, skirting the edge of the mud. I dived for dry ground and made it just as he came around. He thrust the rifle bayonet forward. I sidestepped his lunge, grabbed the rifle barrel and gave him a karate blow alongside the neck. He gasped, and I wrenched the rifle from him, spun it around and fired. The damn thing misfired, and I had to give him another chop in the same place. He toppled over.

I turned to see that the third man had clambered down from the porch and was racing for me, his machete upraised. I fired at point-blank range, but he kept coming. The damned rifle was either misfiring again or the ammo was bad. I dropped to both knees, to avoid being beheaded by a wild swing of the machete. This time I didn't bother firing but brought the rifle up to parry a short, chopping blow. I was on my back, and as the machete hit the rifle, I kicked up and out, catching the Vietnamese in the belly. He doubled over, and I swung the rifle stock up against his jaw. I felt the bone shatter as the heavy stock smashed into his face, and he collapsed.

I got up and fired the rifle again, into the dirt this time. Again nothing happened. I threw the thing away and looked around. The paratroopers were pushing the defenders back toward a small wooden hut in the center of the village. It appeared to be the heart of the enemy's defense, and I wagered that the senator and his party were inside it. The battle had turned into something near a slaughter; the ground was littered with the bodies of dead Vietcong and the renegade regulars. I grabbed another rifle from one of the dead VC, ducked around one of the huts and headed for the rear of the central hut. I found half-a-dozen defenders there. They opened fire as I came into view, and I hit the dirt. I fired back in short bursts with the Russian-made automatic rifle. They continued to shoot, missing me, but I wasn't doing any better and I wondered if it was because I was unused to the action of the rifle.

I heard someone running behind

me, turned to see two paratroopers come up, and with one burst, cut down the six defenders. They ran on and I got to my feet, frowning, annoyed with myself. Even with a strange rifle I wasn't that bad a shot. I fired a short burst into the side of the wooden hut. Once again, nothing happened, and now I understood: the rifle was loaded with dummy cartridges—blanks.

The first one I'd tried to use must also have been loaded with blanks, and now I saw why the battle was so one-sided. The poor bastards were probably all using blanks. It wasn't unheard of in guerrilla operations of this kind. They sometimes grabbed test ammunition on a hit-run raid, thinking they had the real thing. But it didn't happen that often either. It was a strange, bizarre note that gave me a distinctly uneasy feeling for some reason.

The firing was sporadic now, mainly a few pursuit parties in the surrounding jungle. I went up the steps of the central hut. Major Dreiser was standing in the doorway, a big grin on his face. He ushered me inside where, in a corner of a large, relatively empty room, soldiers were cutting free three unkempt, disheveled figures.

The first one I recognized at once as Senator Atkins, despite a heavy growth of beard. His lined face showed his relief, and he smiled at me as I came in. Beside him, Ferris Dickson was rubbing his wrists and flexing his arms. I'd never seen the senator's aide and protégé before, except in news photos. He was tall, slender and, even with his growth of stubble, a boyish-looking man with a trifle to much haughtiness in his expression to suit me.

One of the troopers finished untying the girl, Judy Howell. She was in jeans and a soiled green shirt, her hair disheveled and matted, her face dirty, smudged, but underneath it all a very pretty girl with a saucy nose, determined chin and bright, brown eyes. The shirt was loose fitting but, even so, her breasts thrust upwards in a youthful, firm outline, and her buttocks in the jeans were rounded and full.

"The info you fellows gave us was right on the nose, Carter," Major Dreiser said gleefully. I nodded. It had been a fantastically perfect operation. The major confirmed what I guessed, that we hadn't lost a man. He began to herd the senator, his aide and the girl out of the hut.

"I want to get them back to the planes at once," he explained. "There may be more Vietcong in the area. Besides, my orders were to get in and get out fast—and that's what I'm going to do."

"Right, Major," I said. "And if I'm correct in my information, we never even landed."

He signaled he understood and disappeared through the narrow doorway. I lingered behind and gave the hut a fast but practised going over. Bits and pieces of clothing, some dry rice kernels, a small bamboo fan littered the floor. There was nothing of value, and I poked into the corners without unearthing anything more than a centipede.

I was on my way out, strolling toward the door, when I saw the small piece of paper partially sticking out of a crack between the floorboards. I knelt down and pulled it free. It was the claim half of a laundry ticket, and I frowned as I gazed at it. The number was 764; the laundry was the Han Laundry in Georgetown, Washington D.C.

The laundry ticket was a helluva long way from home. I pocketed it, wondering which of the three it belonged to as I picked my way across the body-littered ground outside. I heard the sound of engines turning, saw sunlight glinting off the wings of the C-47 lined up on the shorestrip. I broke into a run and was the last man aboard the lead plane. The door slammed behind me, and we were airborne in seconds.

Things had gone perfectly, and everyone was busy congratulating everyone else, especially Major Dreiser. Why the hell was I so inexplicably disturbed? Nothing that couldn't logically be explained had occurred. It had been a smooth, efficient operation,

made easier by a defending force fighting with faulty equipment. But I am
always suspicious of things that go too
easily; maybe that was what bothered
me. For now, I set aside my vague uneasiness and joined the others in congratulating the major.

II

Major Dreiser had set a corner of the plane aside for me where we could interrogate the senator and his party. The major introduced me as a special agent from AXE, and I sat back to let him run the show.

The C-47 had been stripped of every nonessential item to make room for the paratroopers. The senator and the others had to sit on the floor. There was no soap, only a water fountain of cold water at the rear of the aircraft, and the wet towel Judy Howell had rubbed across her face only managed to smear the grime over a wider area.

The senator's lined face, always somewhat haggard-looking, reflected the
ordeal less than that of his two com-
panions. He talked, and Judy Howell
and Ferris Dickson, flanking him,
confined their comments to an occasional nod or brief interjection.

When I sat down beside the major, I
had a paper cup of cold water in hand.
I offered it to the senator. He smiled
gratefully but declined. "No, thank
you, Mr. Carter," he said. "I'll have
some later, perhaps."

"You say you were brutally treated,
Senator," the major prodded.

"It was torture, gentlemen, absolute
torture," Senator Atkins said. "We
were beaten regularly. We were given
nothing to eat but dry rice and driven
nearly mad with thirst. We were questioned incessantly about everything
that popped into their minds. Of
course, they thought we had more information than we actually did."

"You're frowning, Mr. Carter,"
Judy Howell said suddenly. I looked
up and saw her watching me closely.
"Do you find this difficult to believe? I

assure you it's all too true."

The frown had appeared automatically without my realizing it. I shook my head, said quickly, "No, not at all, Miss Howell." She was obviously a very sharp chick. My response was not insincere; it wasn't completely true, either. Actually, I felt the senator was telling the truth, and yet I'd seen men who had been nearly driven insane with thirst. I'd experienced it myself. The victims drank prodigious amounts of water for weeks and weeks afterward. Even if they only sipped at it, water was something they could not refuse. Yet the senator had declined my offer of a drink of water. It was a small thing, perhaps, but it stayed. Long ago I learned never to overlook the small things.

I watched all three as they told their stories with obvious emotional sincerity. They looked tired, all of them, and they were plainly telling of things that had happened to them. *Only?* That word again. I couldn't shake it. *Only— what?* Judy Howell was talking, and I leaned forward intently. The loose shirt rose and fell rhythmically and I had all I could do to concentrate on what she was saying instead of the delightful thrust of her full breasts. There was a lovely treasure to be found under that loose shirt, I was certain.

"They kept talking about doing terrible things to me," Judy Howell said, and she shuddered, her shoulder quivering. "They would keep me on the floor naked and come in and stand over me and tell me all the awful, horrible things they were planning. It was terrible . . . just terrible. Sometimes they hit me. Sometimes they just ran their hands over me." She shuddered again. Like the others, she was recounting painful things, and her voice broke with emotion, her saucy, pert face looked strained.

I listened as Ferris Dickson told of his ordeal, of threats and beatings, of being forced to stay awake night and day to the point of exhaustion. As he spoke, his voice, too, grew tense with barely controlled emotion.

These people were bundles of nerves

and tension as they told of their experiences. Why the hell wasn't I satisfied? What was adding to my distinct uneasiness? I watched the senator's eyes as he listened to Dickson, grave, intelligent, serious eyes, and I switched to Judy Howell to take in her bright, alert gaze, and suddenly I knew one of the things that was bothering me: their eyes.

I'd seen men who had been saved from ordeals such as these three described. Their eyes were haunted, filled with unspeakable fears, eyes that have seen more than they want to remember. None of these three had that look. Their words and the emotions they exhibited when they spoke were in order, but their eyes did not match their stories. Something was not right here, I decided. I hadn't the damnedest idea *what* wasn't right, but something wasn't, that was sure.

Major Dreiser was speaking now, and I brought my attention back to the questioning. "That sums it all up for me, Mr. Carter," the major said, turning toward me. "We'll prepare press releases . . . unless you have any questions you want to ask?"

I saw Judy Howell watching me. Maybe it was the defiant tilt of her chin, the somewhat challenging look in her eyes that did it, but I decided I might as well be a bastard openly. Besides, I didn't feel diplomatic. Too many little things were adding up to a big worry inside me. I plunged in.

"I'd like a truth serum test made before any press statements are released on this," I said quietly. I saw Major Dreiser's eyebrows shoot skyward and Ferris Dickson's jaw drop, but it was Judy Howell's voice that broke the stunned silence.

"I don't believe you," she snapped.

"Believe me," I said, quietly. "I mean it."

Ferris Dickson pulled his jaw back up and his face clouded as he followed Judy Howell's lead.

"Now, hold on here," he said. "That's a helluva thing to suggest."

"Mr. Carter is suggesting we're all liars," Judy Howell cut in. She was angry as a hornet, her pretty jaw clenched and her eyes blazing. It was her eyes which hardened my stand. By rights they should be dull, lifeless—not blazing.

"I'm not suggesting anything," I said evenly.

"You certainly are," she shot back. "You're implying this is all some kind of publicity stunt."

I didn't want to make a big issue of it. I hadn't anything concrete to work with. I was going along on past experience and an inner hunch. I tried to smooth it over.

"I'm not implying any such thing," I said, keeping my voice even. "It's pretty much routine, Miss Howell."

She wasn't buying. "It's not at all routine and you know it," she snapped.

"I go along with that," Ferris Dickson chimed in, his expression somewhat petulant. "It's highly unusual."

"This entire affair is highly unusual," I countered.

It was Senator Atkins who interrupted, and I had to give him credit.

Perhaps he was just smarter than the others, or perhaps his years of senatorial warfare had given him a broader perspective.

"Please, Ferris . . . Judy," he said, gravely regarding me. "Let's not get carried away. I know something of Mr. Carter's reputation in his own special work. I'm sure he has some considered reasons behind his request."

I was determined to keep it all matter-of-fact.

"Thank you, Senator," I said. "It's merely that we have found that under sodium pentothal a person's subconscious mind takes over, and the details and impressions imprinted in the subconscious are often of greater importance than those one consciously recalls. It's as simple as that."

The senator nodded, his silver hair falling partly down over his lined face. "I'm perfectly willing to go along with your request, Mr. Carter," he said. "We're in your hands." I shot a glance at Ferris Dickson and the girl. Their closed, somewhat sullen faces told me they were bowing to the senator's lead but not happily.

The question period ended. I started to go back to the rear of the plane, and I found Judy Howell blocking my way.

"I just want you to know that I'm not buying one word of that 'subconscious impression' crap you fed the senator," she said, her brown eyes halfmoons of dark fury.

"Tsk, tsk. Such language," I said.

"Never mind my language," she snapped. "Before becoming a correspondent for *Tomorrow,* I worked on a newspaper. You may be a big wheel in the counterespionage world, but you're a lousy judge of whether people are telling the truth or not."

"Maybe." I grinned down at her. "And you may be a big wheel in the women's magazine world, but you don't know a damn thing about the subtler aspects of modern international intrigue."

"You wait," she said her lower lip shoved out belligerently. "I'm looking forward to seeing your face *after* your truth serum test."

"And I'm looking forward to seeing your face without the dirt all over it, and your hair combed. You might be a good-looking dish."

She clamped her jaws together, turned on her heel and walked away. I stood grinning after her.

We landed at Taipei, transferred to an Air Force jet and flew back to Washington immediately. Everything was still very hush-hush. We landed in the early morning hours, and the military had cars waiting to whisk Senator Atkins and his party to a guarded suite at Walter Reed Hospital. I had radioed Hawk and told him what I'd done, and he was at the airport to meet me. As we drove back to AXE headquarters together, I gave him a more detailed briefing.

"I hope you have some solid basis for this," he commented grimly, his steel-gray eyes disapproving. "Asking someone of Senator Atkins' stature to submit to a sodium pentothal test is a pretty nervy bit, N3. But then you are a nervy bastard, so it doesn't really surprise me."

"It's part of my charm," I said. "I'm irrepressible."

"I hope this charm demonstration doesn't put all our heads on a block," he countered.

"It won't," I said, with somewhat more confidence than I really felt. "I think I've sold the senator on my reasons for it."

"But I presume you have something better than that," he said.

"Maybe."

"Don't be coy with me, N3," Hawk growled.

I grinned. The old fox knew me too well. "I know better than that, Chief," I said. "But give me until tomorrow, after the tests are finished. Then I'll lay the whole thing out for you."

He grunted consent and sat gazing out the window until we reached AXE headquarters.

I spent the night in one of the half-dozen rooms AXE maintains for overnight guests. I keep a small apartment in Washington, but I was too tired to go to it that night. In the morning I slipped out early, made a fast trip to Georgetown and then stopped at my apartment for a moment.

My phone answering service told me that a Miss Linda Smythe had called . . . three times. I returned the call and found Linda wanted me for the coming weekend at her place. It was damned inviting.

"Where have you been all week?" Linda asked. "What exciting things do you have to tell me?"

"None," I said. "A dull business trip." It was a routine Linda and I had perfected long ago. She asked the question, knowing I wouldn't tell the truth, and I gave her the answer, knowing she wouldn't believe me. She giggled.

"You can come, can't you, Nick?" she asked.

"Providing the boss doesn't cancel me out," I said.

"He'd better not. I'll meet you at the station Thursday night, sweetie," she said. "Bye, now."

I hung up with the pleasant anticipation of a nice, relaxed weekend ahead. Linda was more than enough to look forward to but believe it or not, it was more than that. I like to ride. It has always been a relaxing sport to me and I don't get the chance often enough. I made a note on the calendar pad beside the phone: "Weekend—Thursday night—Linda Smythe."

I checked out Wilhelmina, my faithful and favorite Luger, slipped her into the shoulder holster and tightened one of the bands on Hugo's holster. The pencil-thin stiletto, resting in its leather sheath strapped to my forearm, had saved my life more times than I cared to remember.

The sodium pentothal was being administered when I reached the hospital. Hawk was there with a tape recorder and so was Major Dreiser. I'd asked him to do the questioning. I wanted the same general pattern as on the plane. A press conference announcing the rescue had been set up for later, allowing enough time for the drug to wear off.

I grimaced as the truth-serum brought out nothing new. All three of the subjects repeated the same basic statements they had originally made, including the senator's remark about being driven nearly insane with thirst. When the tests were over, Hawk snapped the small tape recorder shut and we went into an anteroom to wait for the senator and the others.

Hawk stared at me and sighed. When the senator appeared, followed by Ferris Dickson and Judy Howell, Hawk took the ball with the air of a parent having to extricate a delinquent child from an unhappy predicament he had gotten himself into. The senator's eyes reflected sincere concern. Ferris Dickson looked sullen, and Judy Howell's eyes glowed with controlled anger.

During the tests, she had been on a hospital bed, a light sheet over her, the room semi-darkened. Now I saw that she was wearing a cerise silk blouse and a white skirt, the blouse clinging provocatively in all the right places. Her legs were smooth and lovely, I noted, and her face pert and alert under short, brown hair. Without the grime and dirt, her skin glowed. She was a thoroughly attractive little piece, I decided.

"I'm happy to tell you that there were no changes of any significance during the test," Hawk announced, his lean, leathery New England face breaking into a smile of utter charm. I'd seen it happen a few times before and I always marveled at how very suave he could be when he felt like it, or more correctly, when he felt it was needed.

"I want to thank you all for cooperating with us as you have," he went on. "It's most helpful to us in our work, though this may be difficult for you to completely understand. So, please accept our gratitude."

He and Major Dreiser escorted the senator from the room, making small talk. Dickson trailed them and I found myself alone with Judy Howell.

"You don't know how happy this makes me," she said smugly.

"Me too." I smiled. "I found out exactly what I wanted to know."

She frowned. That threw her a little; it wasn't what she'd expected. She

tried again, coming in from a different
tack.

"I hate people who can't trust anyone," she said flatly.

"So do I," I said, holding her eyes
with mine. She frowned again, realizing she'd been hit with her own shaft.

"You're clever, Mr. Carter," she
said, gazing at me, eyes narrowed,
their expression speculative. I already
knew she was alert and sharp. I found
out now she was more than ordinarily
perceptive.

"You know something else, Mr.
Carter?" she said. "You're not letting
go yet, are you? You're still not satisfied."

My smile was slow and a little nasty. I was annoyed that she read me so
well.

"I'm never satisfied, Miss Howell,"
I told her. "It's a flaw in my person-
ality."

Her eyes narrowed further, in disbelief. "Now it's my turn not to buy,"
she said.

"Whatever you say." I shrugged.
"I'm a very agreeable fellow. And I'm

glad I was so right."

"About what?" she snapped, flaring instantly.

"About what nice things were underneath all that grime and the sloppy clothing."

Her eyes stayed on me, studying me. "I think I'd like a long talk with you," she said. "Could that be arranged?"

"You can count on it, honey," I said, and walked out of the room. Judy Howell had been more right than she knew. I don't let go of things, not easily, anyway, and I wasn't letting go of this.

I went out and had lunch. It gave me more time to organize my thoughts before facing the chief. When I arrived back at AXE offices on DuPont Circle, Hawk had already returned and was waiting for me. I sat down across the desk from him, noting the tape recorder on the table nearby. Hawk's eyes were flint and his face immobile. I knew the signs. He was annoyed.

"I'm waiting, N3," he said. "I want to know what you have that makes you

subject probably the most powerful
senator in America to a truth serum
test. We won't even mention his right-
hand aide and a very scrappy, snoopy
special magazine correspondent."

"Just being thorough, Chief," I
said. "Just doing the kind of a job you
want us to do."

"You can cut out the humility, N3,"
Hawk grimaced. "It's out of character."

I grinned, nodded. "Okay, you're
right," I said. "I took the risk, chief,
because I'm bothered. There's something wrong about this whole affair. It
makes clunking noises to me. I can't
give you anything really tied together,
though."

"Give me what you've got untied,"
he grunted.

"Starting from the beginning," I
began, "the whole thing had a funny
feel to it. The operation went off too
damned well. The Vietcong irregulars
were annihilated because their rifles
held blank ammo. I'm convinced of
it. I tested two of the rifles myself—"

"You know that's logically possible,

Nick," Hawk interrupted. "Those ragtag outfits often get hold of dummy ammo and think it's the real thing. Sometimes it's sold to them by fast-buck merchants."

"I agree there, Chief," I said. "But then later on, in the C-47, I offered the senator a cup of water, and he declined. Yet you heard what he said about how they were driven nearly insane with thirst. You've seen men who've been without water for a long time."

"Yes," he said thoughtfully. "They can't get enough to drink. It's an interesting point. But you can't think they made it all up. The truth serum test destroyed that idea, Nick."

"I know, but I still say it doesn't fit right," I said. "I say what happened is not exactly what they say happened. I say that's only in their minds. They *think* that they were driven mad by thirst. They're convinced of it and it's real to them. They're not lying. That's why their stories held up under the sodium pentothal. But their physical reactions don't bear out what they say. The mind can be made to believe anything, but the body reacts independently. When the senator refused the water I offered, it was a natural physical reaction. His body didn't need a drink of water. It wasn't really dehydrated."

"I want to chew on that a while, N3," Hawk said. "Anything else?"

"This," I answered, tossing the laundry ticket on the desk in front of him. He stared at it for a moment, then gave me an exasperated look.

"Kindly spare me the suspense bit." He sighed. "What connection does a laundry ticket have with this?"

I leaned back. "I found it inside the hut where the senator and the others had been held captive," I said. "I thought it no doubt belonged to one of them but when I checked it out, surprise, surprise. It belongs to a character named Samuel Sonyoung."

Hawk's eyes were flicking back and forth now, and I could almost hear his mind clicking.

"Who, pray tell, is Samuel Sonyoung?"

I shrugged. "That's one I don't know, yet. But the laundry did tell me where he lives. Seventeenth Avenue, Georgetown, near the waterfront. I thought maybe Vital Statistics might have something on him."

Hawk reached for the intercom. "We'll get them on it immediately," he said. "You never know what they have in that card system of theirs."

Vital Statistics did indeed have a helluva file index on an awful lot of people. Most of them, however, either had some inter-governmental connection, were in foreign agencies of one sort or another or had had some brush with official law agencies which would result in a listing for them. Of course, international operatives were also on file. That index took in the big and the little fish, from heads of espionage activities to lowly clerks. But if Samuel Sonyoung didn't fall into one of those categories they wouldn't have a card on him.

When he'd finished with the intercom, Hawk leaned back, touching the fingertips of his hands together meditatively.

"What is a ticket from a laundry in Georgetown doing out in North Vietnam, at the compound where Senator Atkins was held?" he asked aloud. He was giving voice to what he knew I had asked myself.

"Most interesting," he went on. "And most disturbing. The next step is to find out who this Samuel Sonyoung is. I presume you've scheduled a visit to him?"

"Soon as I leave here," I said.

"Got anything else?" Hawk asked, his gaze speculative. "Any ideas what this could mean? You don't really smell a publicity stunt, do you, Nick? Not a man of Senator Atkins' stature. He doesn't go in for grandstand personal publicity exploits the way some of the others do. He has no need for them."

"He could have been talked into one," I ventured.

"By the magazine correspondent?" Hawk asked. "Or, by Ferris Dickson for his own reasons? Possibly, but I'd very much doubt it. Senator Atkins just isn't the man for it."

"I agree, Chief," I said. "I don't know what it all might mean. I only know I feel there's something very rotten somewhere in this. I feel it in my bones."

I didn't voice it then, but there was something strangely sinister in it, something far, far beyond any publicity stunt. I had the feeling of dark and evil forces at work, and I wasn't one for schoolboy dramatics.

"All right, N3," Hawk said, standing up. "Follow it through. This is an increasingly strange world we live in, and you've come up with some interesting facts that only a nasty, suspicious mind like yours could do anything with."

I grinned at him. "You say such nice things," I said. "I'll try not to let it go to my head."

Hawk snorted, turned to the window and I knew it was time for me to take off.

I stopped off at my place for a hot shower. I often do some of my best thinking under the shower. I wrestled with the best way to approach this Samuel Sonyoung. The shower didn't do the job this time, because when I finished dressing I was still wrestling with the problem.

I was about to leave when the phone rang, the blue one in my desk drawer that was a direct line to Hawk. His voice came over terse, brisk.

"A bit of luck, perhaps, Nick," he said. "Statistics had a card on a Professor Samuel Sonyoung. Not much of a card but at least it's something. A Professor Samuel Sonyoung taught at Craymoor College a few years ago when he was brought into court on a morals charge. The charge was finally dropped and he was later dismissed from his teaching post. His subject was Comparative Philosophy. Now, where does that fit into this?"

"No place at all," I said. "But it's good to know. The more you know, the smarter you are."

Hawk grunted and hung up. Craymoor College was a small, fairly exclusive women's college in the District of Columbia. The item itself told me nothing much. Possibly it wasn't the same character, though I doubted there were too many Samuel Son-young's running about. But it did give me an idea for an approach. I had borrowed an AXE car, and as I drove out to Georgetown, I decided on a wide-eyed, somewhat breathless characterization.

The house on Seventeen Avenue turned out to be a renovated brownstone, well-kept in an otherwise dingy neighborhood. I parked a few houses away and walked to the front door, quickly spotting the name on the bell. It was a ground-floor apartment and the buzzer admitted me through the front door. At the right of a small, neat hallway, an apartment door opened and a man poked his head out. He was an Oriental, perhaps Korean or Vietnamese. It was hard to tell. It was harder yet to tell his age, but I guessed him anywhere from 35 to 45. Fairly tall, he had a small, indecisive beard that did little more than grace his chin with a few hairs. He wore a

Mao shirt and black silk Oriental trousers, short and wide in cut.

"Mr. Sonyoung?" I said, putting just a touch of hesitation in my voice, a dash of timidity.

"Yes," he said evenly.

"I have something that belongs to you," I said, standing before him. I handed him the laundry ticket, thrusting it at him. I thought I saw his eyes flicker for an instant.

"Why, thank you," he said, looking up at me pleasantly. "I had wondered what had become of it. Where did you find it?"

"On the street some weeks ago," I said. "Unfortunately I had to go away on business, and I didn't return until yesterday. They wanted to keep it for you at the laundry, but I insisted on returning it to you myself when I heard your name."

His eyebrows lifted gravely. "And why was that?"

"I wondered if you were the Professor Sonyoung my niece had some years ago at Craymoor College," I said, keeping the breathlessness in my voice.

He smiled again, a slow, controlled smile. "I would presume so," he said. "I did teach at Craymoor."

"By gosh," I exclaimed. "I've so wanted to meet you, Professor. Mary Ann used to tell me about the fascinating things you discussed during your class. Do you remember her, Mary Ann Howes? Small, dark-haired girl, kind of timid?"

Sonyoung shook his head. "I'm afraid not Mr.—?"

"Franklin," I said. "Dan Franklin. Mary Ann used to tell me that you were the most interesting teacher she ever had."

Sonyoung smiled, a little smugly. I'd touched his ego, apparently. He stepped back and opened the door wider.

"Please," he said with a half-bow. "Won't you come in? It was most kind of you to take the trouble to return the laundry ticket. Very few people are so thoughtful."

He hadn't an accent, but there was a faint slur to his speech on certain words. I noticed his eyes, small and dark, studying me with veiled amusement as I walked into the apartment. My eyes swept the room with a practiced glance, seeking the things I wanted to find first. There was but one closed window. I glimpsed another room beyond, a bedroom. Chances were it had a window. The only other way in was the front door.

I glanced around the rest of the room. It was cluttered with papers and books. One wall held a double row of bookshelves. A desk with a typewriter on it and a lamp nearby took up the far end of the room. Two chairs and a small table, all loaded with books and notes, filled out the rest of the room.

Sonyoung crossed the room to his desk, walking on the tips of his feet. There was a spring, a graceful strength to his walk that made me conclude he no doubt practiced some form of judo or wrestling.

"Will you have a drink, Mr. Franklin?" he asked. "A little Scotch, perhaps?" His eyes continued to regard me with hidden amusement. He was smooth, very self-contained. But there was a quality to him, an air of intensity held back by sheer willpower. His eyes probed and searched with a strange ominousness. He was one of those men who could both disturb and fascinate others. I wondered about the morals charge, how valid it had been. Valid enough, I concluded. I declined the offer of a drink with thanks.

"What do you do, Mr. Franklin?" he asked politely.

"I'm a salesman," I said. "Wholesale jewelry."

I watched that slow, controlled smile crawl across his face again. I found myself wondering if that smile didn't stand for a great deal more than politeness. I turned, aware he was watching me, and looked across the row of books on the nearest shelf. Three titles had to do with psychic phenomena, two with the power of the mind and one with drugs.

"Are you interested in psychic phenomena, Mr. Franklin?" he asked.

"Good gosh, no," I said, maintaining my air of naive awe. "I'm not smart enough for any of that. I only wish I could be. You said that you *did* teach at Craymoor? Does that mean you're not there anymore?"

"Not anymore," he answered. "I ... er ... left there about two years ago."

"Golly, I'll have to tell Mary Ann next time I see her," I said. "You teaching somewhere else now?"

"No," he said, smiling pleasantly. "I have a modest income from my scientific writings and lecturing."

I turned. It was time to exit. I'd seen enough to know I had to get back in there alone. This cluttered apartment, I was convinced, had things to reveal. Besides, I could overplay my little bit, if I wasn't careful.

"I'd like to stay but I can't," I said. "I just wanted to meet you. Mary Ann will be excited when I tell her I did."

Sonyoung nodded. "I appreciate your thoughtfulness in returning the laundry ticket. Do come by again sometime when you can stay."

I professed eager willingness and left. I could sense his eyes following me down the hall and I wondered whether my little act had taken him in. He was undoubtedly a shrewd cookie.

It was dark outside, and I moved the car to the other side of the street where I could have an unobstructed view of the brownstone. I wanted into that apartment badly. Sonyoung fitted perfectly with the strange, sinister quality of this entire bit. Just how he fitted was something I very much wanted to discover. If my luck held out I might be on the verge of it.

It did. Just past eight o'clock, I saw a slender figure, now dressed in western clothes, suit coat, a hat pulled low over the face, emerge from the building. Sonyoung paused under a streetlamp, and I saw the thin line of his beard. He walked off with a fast, easy stride, and I watched him till he was out of sight. I gave him a few minutes more and than went into action.

The basement of the brownstone led

into the courtyard, and I could see the two windows of Sonyoung's ground-floor apartment just above me. There were plenty of ledges and architectural protrusions on the building and climbing up was easy enough. Both windows were locked, however, I decided to force the bedroom window. Clinging to the window sill, I couldn't get much leverage as I strained at the window. Luckily, the wood of the window frame was old and rotted. The lock gave way under steady pressure, and I found myself in the bedroom. It was sparsely furnished with only a chair beside the bed.

I went into the living room, switched on the lamp and began a fast but thorough search of the place. I took the closets first, going through the pockets of his suits. I was hunting for some evidence that would nail down his presence in North Vietnam sometime during the past month or so. I hoped, perhaps, for a plane ticket or a baggage stub but there was nothing. He had luggage in a closet but it was clean of all stubs or stickers.

I went through the desk, drawer by drawer, coming across a small volume entitled "Mind Manipulation" by S. Sonyoung. I gave it a quick examination and found it was a detailed study of brainwashing techniques. The professor, it appeared, had a very thorough knowledge of the subject. A whole drawer of envelopes revealed that he kept up a steady correspondence with people in India and other Asian countries. The envelopes were all empty return mail envelopes.

It was in the bottom drawer that I found the loose manuscript pages. The title caught me immediately:

"THE TECHNIQUE OF MIND CONTROL
AS DEVELOPED BY S. SONYOUNG"

The manuscript was plainly the opening pages of something he was working on and the text, neatly typed, leaped out at me with an almost live urgency.

"The control of man's mind is with us," I read. "And man, himself, has set the very pattern for that control.

By mind control I do not mean brainwashing. This is but a minor adjunct in mind control. Brainwashing is to condition the brain to think as you wish it to think. Mind control is to condition the mind to act as you wish it to act.

"Man acts in accordance with the impulses that go through his mind, just as a computer acts in accordance with the data that goes through its brain cells. The computer itself has been patterned after a simplified version of man's own mental processes. It is ironically fitting that man's mind can now be patterned after the principles of computer programming. This is the heart of the Sonyoung Mind Control Technique.

"The modern computer stores information in its memory cells and, when tapes with the correct codes are fed into it, those memory cells are instantly activated. When another set of coded data is fed into the computer, another set of memory cells is activated. In this manner, the computer is programmed to respond with certain information on command.

"The mind of man can be equally programmed to respond on command. Properly conditioned beforehand, the mind can be made to respond automatically to any code or signal which has been prefixed in its mental circuits. The mind, therefore, can be transformed into a computerized mental circuit paralleling the electronic or binary circuits of the computer . . .

"One of the important factors in this process of computerizing the mind for controlled response is the normal resistance of the mind to control. To lower this resistance and make the mind more receptive, the mind must be kept preoccupied with artificially produced stress. During such artificially produced stress, anxieties and fears occupy the conscious mind, making the subconscious more receptive to imprinting.

"This is accomplished by a highly complex technique, which includes the use of mind-expanding hallucinogenic drugs, administered while the subject is unconscious, psychological pressures to the conscious mind, advanced posthypnotic techniques and repeated subliminal implementation. It could be looked upon as a modern, mind-oriented version of the ancient carnival gambler's trick with three shells and a pea. He keeps his audience watching one thing while he is actually doing another. So the conscious mind is kept preoccupied with certain things while something else is happening to the subconscious mind. Because of the very nature of the mind, a mind so programmed must respond to the code or signal just as completely as the computer responds to the tape fed into it. It has become a controlled mind, subject to a programmed response determined by the controller . . ."

I put down the papers and stared at the typed lines, unseeing, my mind racing. Mind control had always been a particularly reprehensible concept to me. It destroyed those things man had struggled to build since he emerged from the slime and ooze of primordial times—his own mind, his free will, his intellectual capability to

make considered judgments. Strip
that from man and he becomes a big
two-legged laboratory rat, acting only
on the basis of emotional stimuli or
outside control. If Sonyoung's partially completed paper could be believed,
he had found a way to do just that,
turn man into a flesh-and-blood computer, his acts governed by someone
else.

The paper I'd just read raised a
helluva lot of possibilities, all of them
frightening. The sinisterness I'd felt
about this whole business was taking
on added form and horror. Where did
it all tie in with the capture of Senator
Atkins, Ferris Dickson and Judy
Howell?

I was sure of one thing: Sonyoung
had been in Vietnam at the time the
senator was a prisoner there. The
laundry ticket placed him there, and if
I had any lingering doubts about it,
they had been dispelled by what I'd
just read. The mind-control expert
was involved up to his scrawny little
beard, and he was far from alone in it.

A very nasty but very real fear

struck me. What if Sonyoung and his pals—whoever they were—had planned to program the minds of their three captives? Judy Howell couldn't reveal much, but the senator and his aide possessed a tremendous amount of top-level information America's enemies would love to have.

Our raid had no doubt frustrated that scheme, but what if it were only a beginning, I mused, warming to the thought. What if they had other prominent officials marked for abduction and mind-control programming? Operation Senator, had wrecked their first try, but I was betting that wouldn't stop them.

I was so taken with my own musings, I didn't hear a sound until the doorknob turned. I only had time to kick over the lamp and plunge the room into darkness. As I raced for the bedroom, I glimpsed Sonyoung, the light from the outside hall framing his figure in the doorway. I heard the gun bark as I reached the window, felt the slug tear past my ear and into the wall. I vaulted over the window ledge and dropped, bending my knees in an effort to cushion the shock of the fall. But it was a good drop, and it shook my teeth as I landed. The bottoms of my feet stung like hell. The court, thank God, was pitch-black and, though Sonyoung got off another shot from the window, I was only a barely discernible dark blur. I made the street and the car without further difficulty. As I roared off, I wondered if he had recognized me when he entered the apartment. Even so, I reasoned, I was just a guy named Dan Franklin. It wouldn't make much difference.

That was just one of my mistakes that night.

I drove back to my place, turning what I'd discovered over in my mind. I pretty well knew what they were planning, I was convinced. What I had to do was find out who they had marked for their next victim, prevent them from carrying out their next plan and then nail them. I had nothing on Sonyoung as yet. Nothing at all but my own convictions of what was going on. I had to get concrete evidence.

Sonyoung's mind control techniques were the key to the entire operation. They were to be applied to important figures to obtain vital, secret information. The victims' minds were to be programmed to respond with the answers to any questions put to them. I felt a little smug and self-satisfied with my analysis—which only proves that one can be so right and so wrong at the same time.

In the morning I paid a call on Hawk and briefed him on what I'd found out about Samuel Sonyoung. He sat back, lips tight.

"You believe this mind control is a real possibility, N3?" he asked.

"If Sonyoung has really developed the mechanics of it, I believe it's more than possible," I said.

"Then, going along with your idea of what they are planning, it's also possible that they'll make another attempt on Senator Atkins, or Ferris Dickson, or both."

I nodded, though it was a thought I hadn't included in my own estimate of their next move.

"The senator is giving a big return-home party next Tuesday night at his place," Hawk said. "I'd guess damned near most of official Washington will be there. So will you. I'll see that an invitation is sent to you today."

"Make it two," I said. "It'd look better, less official."

"All right, you have a point there," he said. "I just wish I were sure it was your real reason."

I left Hawk, paid a call on an old friend in the Washington Police Department, Bill Williams, now an Inspector. I asked him to dig up whatever he could on the Sonyoung morals charge. It turned out that what they had was so sketchy and limited that it was little more than a listing of the charge and the subsequent withdrawal. Bill promised to dig further if he could, and I went back to my place.

The minute I touched the door I knew there was trouble. It swung open and I went in to find the place upside down. A thorough search job had been done. My small apartment in Washington had never been touched before.

Only a few people even knew I had it, and only one name leaped into my mind—Sonyoung. But how the hell did he find out where I lived? Besides, I was Dan Franklin to him, if anybody.

I hadn't been tailed from his place last night. I was certain of it. I'd been plenty alert and watching my rearview mirror is second nature to me on a job. But obviously I had overestimated Professor Sonyoung. But that still didn't explain how the hell he found out who I was and where I lived.

I looked through the disarrayed drawers and closets. Nothing had been taken but everything had been examined. They had been plainly trying to find something which would tell them how much I knew, if anything. I sat down, thinking hard. Who, in this affair, knew I was involved—me, Nick Carter, AXE Agent N3? Hawk, of course. Major Dreiser. Senator Atkins and his aide Ferris Dickson and Judy Howell. That was pretty much it. If anyone had flapped their mouths chances were it was one of the last three. I picked up the phone and found that *Tomorrow* magazine had a Washington bureau. A little surprised, I reached Judy Howell at that number.

"Good morning," she said, a little warily after I told her who was calling. "Are you ready for the long talk I want to have?"

"Not yet," I said, trying to sound very casual and pleasant. "But I do want some answers, if you have them. Has anyone asked you about me during the last twenty-four hours?"

"Why, yes, as a matter of fact," she answered, surprise plain in her voice. "How did you know? It was only a few hours ago when I arrived at the office here."

"I'm psychic," I said grimly. "Tell me what happened."

"A man was here to see me, an Oriental gentleman," she said. "Of course, he'd read in the newspapers after the story broke yesterday that I was involved. He said he was from a Chinese-American News Agency and was doing a story on the rescue. He asked if I could describe the special agent who took part in the rescue, what you looked like, how tall you were and all that sort of thing. He said he was writing a human interest story for Chinese newspapers here."

"And you told him, of course," I said.

"Why, yes," she said. "I didn't see anything wrong with it. I gave him your name."

"You didn't ask to see his credentials or anything silly like that, of course," I said sarcastically.

There was a moment of silence and then she said, her voice very small, "I guess not. Did I do something wrong?"

"Let's just say it's lucky we're not having that long talk now, honey," I answered.

I hung up and cursed all the loose-lipped females in the world. It was simple to follow now. Sonyoung probably hadn't bought my little act in the first place, not entirely, anyway. And he obviously glimpsed enough of the intruder in his apartment to recognize Dan Franklin again. He knew damned well an AXE agent had been involved in Operation Senator, and so he pumped Judy Howell for a description of me.

The minute he got it he knew who Dan Franklin was and with my name, the rest was simple: checking my address in the phone book. I don't go in for the unlisted phone bit. Too many people have contacted me that way with too many valuable leads, people who wouldn't have been able to get to me if I had an unlisted phone.

Things had taken a fast turn in the last few hours. Sonyoung knew now I was onto him and I knew he was onto me. That didn't tell me what their next move would be, and it didn't tell him how much I'd figured out. But it did clarify things—and make the kettle boil a little hotter.

III

I spent the next two days digging into Professor Sonyoung's past and didn't come up with a helluva lot. Claymoor College officials were very close-mouthed and stuffy about him. I would have thrown weight and insisted, but I figured that insisting wouldn't elicit anything but the barest of facts anyway.

None of the airlines had a record of a Professor Samuel Sonyoung booked on any flight during the last month. That didn't prove much; he could have used another name. But that's the procedure: you check out every lead. You get twenty dead ends for one good one.

The most help came from my friend Bill Williams. He found the man, a Sergeant Waters, who had been on the desk at the time Sonyoung was hailed into court. I got a call from the sergeant at Bill Williams' request.

"I remember it," the sergeant said over the phone to me. "It struck in my mind because he had a funny name and because my daughter was looking for a college at the time. I remember thinking how you can pick out a good college and yet somethin' like this can happen."

"It was a morals charge, wasn't it?" I questioned.

"Well, it was and it wasn't," the policeman said. "The girl's parents dropped the charges because of the usual—nobody wanted any publicity, not the girl, not her parents and not the school. The actual complaint was that he took girls to his apartment from his classes and did funny things to them."

"What kind of funny things?"

"They were all very vague about that," the sergeant said. "We got some girls in who testified to the original complaint but none of them ever could make a morals charge. Or maybe they didn't want to. Two of them did say they took their clothes off at his place, but they said that's all they did. They couldn't even say why. Anyway, the whole thing was shelved finally."

"Thanks very much, Sergeant," I said. "Every little bit helps."

And it had helped, in its way. Sonyoung had plainly been perfecting his mind control technique, practicing on his students. How well he'd perfected it was anybody's guess. But I kept seeing that manuscript of his, the words revolving around in a frightening refrain: "The mind of man can be programmed to respond on command. . . . can be transformed into a computerized mental circuit."

Sonyoung was a dangerous man, perhaps more dangerous than any other man alive. If he could make those words come true, he was not only a danger to America and the free world but to all mankind. And he had found backers, it was clear. The Chinese Communists? They would certainly go for his theories and his results. But I had the feeling it was not their play— yet. If, as I was beginning to think, Sonyoung was Vietnamese, he had probably hooked up with a hard-core group of the Vietcong. Such a weapon would give them a bargaining position in the world hierarchy they never dreamed of having.

I was going to stick to playing a waiting game for now, anyway. Sonyoung and whoever was in this with him had to make their move soon. I had to be ready for that move. I was convinced I thoroughly understood the meaning of the manuscript. If only I'd known what it was I was *really* waiting for . . .

On Thursday I told Hawk where I'd be for the weekend—Linda Smythe's estate in Fairfax. I'd already told him of my place being searched, thanks to *Tomorrow* Magazine's ace correspondent. Linda was waiting for me at the railroad station when I got there. Approaching winter was in the air and a cold night was beginning to blow in. Leaves played tag in front of us on the road, as she drove her little Triumph along the winding country lanes. Linda was in slacks and a heavy, woolly sweater that, though it tried, could not hide the full swell of her breasts. She had kissed me lightly when we met, then not so lightly.

"I'm looking forward to a great weekend," she said.

"You're referring to riding," I said.

"Why, of course, riding." She laughed.

It did promise to be a great day for horses and riders coming up. Linda had arranged for a point-to-point over her estate, and Friday we would have a dry run, letting horses and riders familiarize themselves with the course. It would be a leisurely run with no one out to prove anything. The following day, Saturday, would be the real ride, over the same route, of course. One of the great things about Linda's property was that she could lay out four or five courses.

Picking a horse from Linda's stable was usually a matter of first come, first served. Most riders, though, stayed with a horse they liked and I did the same, sticking with a magnificent chestnut with some Arabian in him, a powerful horse, full of spirit and fire. He was big and strong, jumped well and could let out on the flat. Linda always invited good riders and good sportsmen: Terry O'Dell, Ritche Washford, Cynthia Hopkins—all top riders, all a helluva lot better than I was at the finer aspects of horsemanship. They had more time to practice than I did. But I made up for lack of practice with drive and abandon. Ritche Washford once told me, "Nick, old boy, you'd come a cropper at the indoor jumps, but out here in the wide-open spaces you're a damned whirlwind."

Friday dawned clear and bright and invigorating. Most everyone had arrived either Thursday night or early Friday morning, and the ride was a good one in the cold, crisp afternoon sun. Ritche Washford and I played tag

for a while and took most of the jumps
on each other's heels. Cynthia
Hopkins, a tall, dark-haired girl,
stayed close behind with Linda and
the others following.

"Why don't you give up that government thing of yours, whatever it is you
do, and devote yourself to riding,
Nick?" Cynthia asked me at dinner
that evening. "You have won at shows,
I know, but you could really be great,
if you had the time to ride."

I smiled at her. "What I do makes it
possible for all of you to keep doing
what you do," I said. "There are a lot
of people who envy everything that's
good and attractive in your world, and
they're out to change it. They want to
make you all into drones. Somebody's
got to watch them."

"Hear, hear!" Ritche called out, lifting his glass. I'd been half-kidding
with my reply. Cynthia was an ace
mathematician with a big lab. Ritche
Washford had served in an important
Intelligence slot during Korea. They
weren't merely playgirls and play-
boys, this crowd, which is what made

our get-togethers what they were, time spent with people you could like and respect.

As always, at Linda's, dinner was superb, leading off with a chilled shrimp and a delicious remoulade, followed by roast leg of lamb with mint jelly, baked potatoes, stuffed mushrooms and french-style green beans with slivered almonds. A good burgundy, a Chambertin 1961, with the lamb. Of course, the others enjoyed the dinner. They were used to good food and good wines, but as I sat back, I wondered if they could enjoy it as I did. When you've stared down death, when you've seen the twisted hate and ugly filth in this world, and when you know that more of the same is out there waiting for you, you enjoy the good things in a special way, in a way few others can enjoy them.

Later, much later, with Linda beside me, the feel of her long, lean body naked against mine, I could almost forget about Sonyoung and the evil I knew surrounded him. Almost. Linda made purring noises, the soft sounds of a woman who knows she is about to be completely and thoroughly fulfilled.

"Penny for your thoughts, Nick," she said, her wide-cheeked, angular face looking up at me. There was concern in her blue eyes, a hint of a frown between them.

"Not worth a penny," I said.

"Then chase them away," she said, getting up on one elbow and moving so that a breast fitted into my hand. The warmth of my hand on her soft skin communicated a desire that sparked her entire body as a match sparks a fire. She put her hands on my shoulder and pulled me onto her lean, wiry body, holding me there as she pressed her torso upwards and small noises came from her parted lips.

She came to me with a desire I answered, and we were as one, moving as an entity, rising and falling as one body. Her legs, slim and strong, clasped themselves around my hips. As always, when her time came, she tossed her head from side to side on the pillow and gasped in rapture. I held her still for a long moment until, with a deep sigh, like the air escaping from a punctured balloon, she sank back, her eyes closed, lips smiling faintly . . .

We were up early the next morning. It was cloudy and gray and the horses were all fired up in the cold air. Pink and rose brushed through the grayness of the sky, and the trees had just enough leaves on them not to be barren.

My big chestnut kicked up his heels as we waited for everybody to assemble. Ritche Washford, wearing a scarlet riding coat, was ready with a stirrup cup of brandy. The fiery liquid was a warming, welcome taste in the cold dawn air. Ritche swung onto Bombshell, a white mare, a good strong hunter, fast and sturdy.

We had at least eight good jumps in the course. We were sent off, and it was Ritche Washford, Linda and myself over the first jump, a simple hedge. Next came a wood fence, then a triple hedge forming a hogback. A stream came after that and then a stretch of broad, level running ground before the next jump. It was Ritche Washford and myself in the lead then. Linda had fallen behind. The kind of reckless speed we were putting on was not her forte.

I let the chestnut have his head on the flat stretch and we caught Ritche quickly enough. Ritche spurred his horse on, but on the flat my big chestnut had more size and muscle. He stretched those powerful legs, enjoying the freedom of running full out. I touched him and he took the lead in seconds.

The jump coming up was a high stone fence and I set myself for it, wondering if the chestnut wasn't going a little too fast. I was going to rein him in a little when his front right hoof struck the rock. His ankle turned and he almost went down. He dipped but caught himself. I reined him up sharply, hoping we could stop before crashing into the stone wall. A horse with a possibly twisted ankle was not one to take this jump.

As I brought the chestnut up sharply, Ritche Washford flew past me on the white mare. She rose for the jump, and I saw her suddenly pitch forward in a funny sort of action, a midair stumble. She brought her forelegs down stiffly, and Ritche flew through the air in a short arc. I grimaced as the scarlet-coated figure bounded off the edge of the stone wall and disappeared over the other side. The mare hit the stone wall and dropped.

My chestnut had halted a few feet from the wall. I leaped from the saddle as the others reined up. I saw Linda dismounting, a look of horror on her face, as I vaulted the wall. Ritche Washford was alive but hurting bad.

"Leg . . . my leg," he groaned. He also had a deep gash on the forehead.

With the help of two others, I held Ritche still while Linda mounted and raced back to the house. She returned with the station wagon, followed by two grooms with the horse van. Using the stretcher always kept in the stables, we lifted Ritche over the wall and into the station wagon. Someone

sped off to Fairfax Hospital with him.
The two grooms were pulling the inert
form of the mare into the horse van.
She had been killed as she slammed
into the wall.

The hunt had ended abruptly, on a
depressing, horrifying note. I put an
arm around Linda and squeezed. She
looked up at me with tear-filled eyes.
She and the others mounted, but I
stared at the wall, seeing Ritche flash
past me and start to take the jump.
Seeing the mare seem to stumble in
mid-air again, pitching Ritche's
scarlet figure through the air. I'd never
seen a spill quite like it, and it bothered me.

"What is it, Nick?" Linda called.
"Come on."

"I'll be along," I said. "I want to see
if I can find what made that horse fall.
You go on. The others will be expecting you."

I watched her gallop off, then
turned and approached the wall. I
walked slowly, my boots tentatively
probing the ground, seeking some-

thing, anything that might have
caused the mare to stumble and fall. If
a tall piece of wood had been sticking
out she might have kicked it, drawn
her legs up further and that was it. It
took very little to throw a horse off at
the start of a jump. She would have
knocked the wood flat, of course, I reasoned as I slid my feet across the
ground.

I had reached the same distance
from the wall where the mare had
begun her jump when my right boot
caught on something. I lifted my toe
and the wire came up with it, thin but
steel-strong, lying in the short brown-
green grass. I knelt down, took it in my
hand and lifted as I stood up. It
dipped off to the right and the left.

On the right, some fifty yards away,
a cluster of bushes and a small birch
stood together. I lifted the wire, following it along. It led to the bushes where
I found the end of it tightly wrapped
around a two-foot length of wood. I re-
traced my steps, lifting the wire as I
went along, this time following it to the

left where, about a hundred yards
from the jump, a line of trees and
brush stretched from east to west. I
was pretty sure what I'd find, and the
anger was starting to coil in the pit of
my stomach, but I had to be certain.

It was there, of course, the other end
of the wire, also coiled tightly around
another length of wood. I gathered the
wire in, quickly reconstructing what
had happened as I did. Two men, one
at each end of the wire, waiting and
watching. They were after only one
person—yours truly.

All they had to do was wait and
raise the wire, holding it taut from
both ends. It was more than enough to
trip a horse. In fact, the horse would
trip itself by drawing its legs up when
it touched the wire. They had seen me
in the lead, raised the wire to get me.
Only, I had reined to a sudden and unexpected halt. Before they could lower
the wire, Ritche Washford had flashed
by me, and his mare hit the wire. No
wonder she seemed to stumble in midair. The slightest pressure at that mo-

ment was more than enough.

The accident had been no accident at all but a carefully calculated plan to kill me or at least put me out of action. Having gone this far, I had to carry through. I mounted the chestnut, checking out his front ankle first. It seemed all right. I galloped back and took the stone wall in a fast, high jump. There were two more jumps we would have taken and I rode to the first one, dismounted and examined the ground. There was nothing there. I took the jump and went on to the last one, another stone wall, not quite so high as the first one. Here I uncovered another length of wire, lying in the grass just a few feet from the wall. I gathered it in and wrapped it around the first ball of wire. As I'd thought, they hadn't bet their chances of success on only one jump. They had been prepared for another try, if I hadn't been in the lead, or if they hadn't a clear shot at me at the first jump. That meant there must have been four of them, at least. It would have been put down as an accident, neat and simple. They probably intended to return to gather up the wire after dark. Now I had saved them the trouble.

My jaw was set grimly, all my muscles tensed in anger as I mounted and rode back to the house. I gave my horse to the stableboy, went in the side door and straight up to my room and put the wire into my small overnight case. The thing that was bothering me most of all, besides what had happened to Ritche Washford, was how the hell had they known I would be here at Linda's? Only Hawk and Linda knew I was coming for the weekend. Of course, there was always the chance that Linda had told someone who told someone else, and so on. Somehow I didn't go along with that. They learned I was here some other way. And they had to have been here yesterday, watching the ride, noting the jumps that were to be taken in the course. That was simple enough for anyone with binoculars. And slipping away in the excitement after the fall was easy enough too. All eyes would be concentrated on the scene of the accident, as indeed they were.

There was something more. The incident told me that Sonyoung and his friends were more than determined that I be taken out of the picture. They were afraid of what I'd put together and they were getting desperate. That was both a good sign and a bad one. From now on, I'd have to watch myself every minute.

When I went downstairs, the hospital had already reported back that Ritche Washford had a fractured tibia, plus some badly pulled tendons and muscles. It would take time, a long time, but it was something that they could fix. He'd be back riding again.

But the incident had cast a pall over the gathering. Dinner was a subdued affair, and most of the group decided to leave early. I had decided against saying anything to Linda about what had really happened. Nothing could be gained by telling her. Besides, I still didn't know how anyone found out I was there. Most of the other guests were people I knew only casually or hardly knew at all. Sonyoung had friends, obviously. Just who they were and where they reached was anybody's guess.

Linda wanted me to stay after the others left. "You don't need to be back till tomorrow, Nick," she pleaded. "We'll be here all alone, just us. No one to bother us." I had to chuckle. The others hadn't bothered us any up to now. But I stayed, and Linda made love that night with an angry determination, as if we could lose ourselves in sex and forget the unpleasantness of the day. It didn't really come off for me, and I don't think it did for Linda either. In the morning I asked Linda to go to the Senator Atkins' homecoming party with me, and she was happy with the idea. I returned to my place Sunday afternoon. I had just walked in the door when it hit me—how Sonyoung's crowd knew where I was for the weekend. Force of

habit. I glanced down at the calendar
pad beside the phone. My handwriting
leaped up at me in the notation I'd
made last week: *Weekend—Thursday
night—Linda Smythe.*

That was it, right there. When
they'd searched my place, they had
seen the message. The rest was simple.
Linda's estate was not exactly an un-
known hideaway, and so finding it
would be no problem. All they had to
do was stay out of sight, observe and
wait their moment.

I debated again about going after
Sonyoung but discarded the idea instantly. I had nothing on him, not really, and I wanted to tear apart the
whole thing. Hawk had said they'd
keep Sonyoung's building under
twenty-four-hour surveillance, anyway, and keep a record of his movements in and out at least.

When I went to bed that night, it
was with the conviction that I had seen
correctly through their plans and that
this was what they feared. More than
that, I had the feeling of an inexorable

chain of events moving toward an inevitable conclusion, of wheels having
been set in motion that were beyond
stopping. Whatever they were planning, they had to go on with it, and I
would be there to meet it head-on.

IV

Hawk had been right about one thing: the senator's party had turned out all of official Washington and a helluva lot of unofficial Washington. Everybody who was anybody was there. Some came because they were really friends of the senator's, truly glad of his safe return. Some came because they felt they ought to, and some because they didn't dare not to.

Linda had arranged to spend the night with Cynthia Hopkins in the city —for the record, at least. We both knew where she really intended to spend it. She looked quite pretty in a blue ruffled formal gown, very femi-

nine and proper. She was instantly at home at the party. She knew
half the people there, which was exactly what I wanted. I hadn't told her this
was more business than pleasure for
me. She was immediately swept up in
dancing and reminiscing with friends,
which gave me a chance to examine
the house.

Even crowded to bursting with people as it was, it was a large, sprawling
place with huge rooms leading off on
both sides from the main dining hall.
A set of terrace doors, open now, led to
the garden. I stepped out on the terrace and saw only a few people,
couples mostly, in the garden. A stone
wall about ten feet high bordered the
property. Cherry and apple trees lined
the wall, and lanterns had been strung
to illuminate most of the area near the
house. Beyond, at the far end, the
garden and the wall disappeared into
darkness with only the light of the
streetlamps reflecting against the
farthest trees. I went back inside, had
a dance with Linda, and then she
danced off with someone else. Drink in

hand, I wandered through every room on the main floor, scanning faces. So far, I saw no one who spelled trouble but that, I knew, didn't mean much. There were a lot of people I hadn't seen yet and a lot more I didn't know. They were just faces but one, or possibly more, of these unidentified faces would attempt something before the night was over.

I decided the best thing would be to stay within range of wherever Senator Atkins happened to be. It wouldn't be possible every minute, but I'd do my best. The senator greeted me heartily, a broad smile on his lined face.

"Glad to see you, Carter," he said, "though I'm told this is a semi official visit . . . that you people are still unhappy about something or other."

I half smiled, apologetically. "We want to take every precaution whenever possible," I said.

"I must say I don't understand this at all," the senator frowned, his eyes grave, concerned. "Especially after that truth serum test to which we were all subjected. I've told you everything

I know. Of course, I want to do all I can to cooperate with you. I am aware of your reputation in this area."

"Much appreciated," I said. "Let's just say that there are some most unusual elements involved which make us feel we should stay in the picture."

He frowned at me. His silver-white hair glistened under the bright lights, and he looked every inch the picture of a United States senator. "That's an answer which really doesn't say anything at all," he protested.

"A technique I learned from listening to senators and politicians in general," I replied.

His smile hesitated a second and then split his lined face. "Good boy," he said, chuckling. "Good luck with whatever you're after. And if you need me for anything, please call on me, Carter. I mean that."

He walked off and I believed him. Senator Herbert Atkins was a man of quality, a man who fulfilled his role in a way few others could claim. My brush with the senator's aide, a minute later, was a very different story. I'd wondered idly why the senator had ever chosen Ferris Dickson to be his confidant and right-hand assistant. Perhaps, like all of us, Senator Atkins was not above flattery and Ferris Dickson was not above flattering. He was not above exercising a sharp, nasty tongue either. Now he sauntered over to me, a flat-chested, hard-eyed blonde on his arm.

"You're like a bad penny, aren't you, Carter?" he said, making no effort to keep the dislike out of his voice. "You keep turning up."

He felt secure in this setting, and his normal snobbish manner took on an added nauseating dimension.

"If it had been up to me, I wouldn't have issued an invitation," he went on. "Even though the request came from high up. I don't normally socialize with people who subject my word to truth serum tests."

"Had it been up to me, I wouldn't be here," I said, keeping my voice pleasant. "The back-biting set holds no attraction for me."

"Exactly why *are* you here,

Carter?" he asked, literally looking down his nose. "Oh, yes, I remember. Something about protecting us from big, bad goblins and things that go bump in the night."

The blonde giggled. I smiled, and Dickson recognized the danger in it. I saw the uncertainty in his eyes. For an instant he thought I might introduce him to a fistful of knuckles. You couldn't trust these raw action types, you know he was thinking. Yes, I would have enjoyed going "bump in the night" on his supercilious smirk.

"Is that why you're here?" The blond giggled again. "Are you really a special agent?"

"I'm a delegate from the W-C-T-U," I told her. "And I'm here to watch the snobs who have nothing to be snobbish about, the social climbers who have nothing to climb with, the ones with ambition and no scruples and those with scruples and no ambition, and the everyday phonies who make up the Washington cocktail set."

"In which one of those charming

categories do I fit?" Ferris Dickson asked thinly.

"I don't know," I said evenly. "Try all five."

The blonde was looking up at him, giving him one of those are-you-going-to-let-him-talk-to-you-that-way looks. He had to make a show of having masculine ego at least.

"Look here, Carter," he said, in his most menacing tone. "I suggest you don't get me angry."

"I suggest you don't get angry," I said. I even smiled when I said it. He got the message. He turned on his heel and left, muttering something to the blonde. He was definitely hostile. Why might be interesting to find out. He could be sore just because of the truth serum test I'd ordered. Or hostility might be a built-in part of his character.

I was turning that over in my mind when a new voice cut into my thoughts. "That was an unfriendly little scene, wasn't it?"

I turned to see Judy Howell at my

elbow. My eyebrows went up at the utter loveliness of her. She was wearing a red evening gown with a white edging on one side in a drape effect. Her breasts spilled out of the V at the top, and her brown eyes were twin dark, sparkling pools.

"Perhaps I should apologize for Ferris," she said, obviously amused.

"Why?" I asked.

"Maybe because I understand the way he feels," she said. "He's not used to having his word doubted, and he's really quite a sensitive young man."

"So am I," I said. "I'm especially sensitive to girl reporters who look like beauty contest winners."

"Thank you," she said, executing a slight curtsy.

"You find gallantry in unexpected places," I told her.

"I'm just doing my job," she said. "These, believe it or not, are my working clothes. As Washington correspondent for *Tomorrow,* I have to cover the doings of Washington society. Besides, as you know, I'm on this special project of covering every day in the life of a senator from the woman's angle."

She moved closer to me, and her sparkling eyes grew serious.

"I've been wanting to talk to you . . . about the other day, about that man who came to see me," she said contritely.

"I know. You want to tell me what makes you talk so much."

"I want to apologize," she said. "I didn't think I was doing anything wrong. I guess it was a little stupid, wasn't it? Did I cause any trouble?"

"Yes, frankly," I told her. "But it's over and done with. At least, that part of it is over."

"I don't suppose I can make up for it," she said, and she was obviously sincere.

"You'll get a chance," I grinned at her. The orchestra started to play, and she moved into my arms. I felt the tips of her breasts press lightly into my chest. The gown, I was happy to discover, was not one of those marvels of engineering and wire buttresses but soft and all her. I let go as the dance ended, reluctantly.

"Don't get carried away by the costume," Judy said, laughing. "I'm still a working girl and I've got to get around and talk to the celebrities. Call me, will you? I still want that long talk . . . more than ever."

I nodded and watched her move off, her bottom round and full inside the red dress, saucy and eminently pattable. I looked around for Linda. She was busy with two handsome young men, chattering away gaily. She caught my eye, gave a small wave and went on chattering. I smiled and looked around next for the senator. I didn't see him, or Ferris Dickson. I didn't even see Judy Howell in the sea of faces.

I was still scanning the room when the shot rang out, one shot, loud and clear, booming over the sound of the orchestra. Some people turned and looked toward the garden where it had come from. Others, unsure of what it was, half-stopped dancing or talking and peered about uneasily. I had no doubt about what it was and I started for the garden.

Getting through the densely packed crowd would take too long. I vaulted over the wooden rail protecting the orchestra and raced around the startled musicians. The crowd, in the way crowds do, had not yet decided how to react. Everybody stayed pretty much where he was. When I reached the garden, a sigh of relief involuntarily escaped me as I saw Senator Atkins bent over a crumpled figure on the terrace floor. Out of the corner of my eye I saw Ferris Dickson, not far from the senator, alone, and a flash of red near the terrace windows was Judy Howell.

The crumpled figure, I saw as I ran around to the other side, was Fillmore Benton, Secretary of the Interior. Others coming out recognized him and started to shout to those inside. "Get a doctor!" someone cried.

Fillmore Benton didn't need a doctor, not anymore. His forehead had been blown half away, and a red stain was covering what was left of his face. It must have been a .357 Magnum at least.

Years of training and experience

governed my moves. I leaped onto a concrete garden bench and, while the others were staring at Fillmore Benton, I scanned the edge of the garden. At the very rear, where there were no lanterns and only the streetlamps cast a glow, I saw a tree move. Someone was climbing it, clambering up the branches that very moment.

"Somebody call the cops!" I yelled and jumped off the bench, heading for the rear of the garden. They were all too transfixed by what had happened to bother about me. The tree was still moving which meant that the climber was still in it. I ran in a straight line, hurdling garden benches as though it were the Olympics.

I reached the trees just as a man's figure, not more than a dark, shadowy shape, dropped out of one of them and poised atop the wall. I clambered up the tree after him and he saw me coming. He paused and I saw his arm lift, heard the shot. I frowned at the sound of it. That wasn't the gun that had killed Fillmore Benton just moments ago. This shot had come from no more than a .22 small-bore handgun, by the sound of it.

He had fired the shot without much aim, more to slow me down. It was a mistake because I kept coming and he lost precious seconds. He dropped over the side of the wall just as I came down out of the tree. Swinging onto the wall, I glimpsed the dark figure racing across the street toward a car, a blue compact model. The street was lined with waiting limousines and their chauffeurs, most of them lounging outside. I dropped over the wall as the engine of the compact roared into life. I raced for the nearest car, a long, gray Imperial. The chauffeur, standing outside, had heard the shot, had seen the man go over the wall and now saw me racing at him. He backed away, fear on his face.

"Where are the keys?" I yelled.

"In-inside . . . in the ig-ignition," he stammered. I jumped in as the blue compact went past. I swung the long car out from the curb and went after him. The limousine was a mixed blessing. It had more than enough power to

stay with the compact and close
ground on the straightaway, but the
fleeing hood quickly learned that it
was a liability on every curve.

He cut across town, taking every
curve he could find. I held the big Imperial on his tail, each curve a paper-
thin brush with lampposts and building walls. Cleverly he stayed away
from main arteries and cut down the
narrow side streets. My palms were
sweating from wrestling the long limousine around each curve. The tires
screamed in protest as the heavy rear
end skidded first to the right, then the
left. The compact kept taking the
curves with only inches to spare itself.

With me, it was only a matter of
time, and the time came on a sharp
right turn into a back street. I felt her
go out from under me, felt the rear end
hit the corner of the building. The
fender crumpled and I heard part of
the bumper rip off. But I'd made it,
and I was still hanging onto the
compact's tail. At the next corner, the
Imperial skidded again, crashing into
the railing of a stoop. The corner after

that was a repeat, only worse. I heard the grinding screech of metal as the rear slammed into the corner of a brick building.

The car's twisted side was now scraping the rear tire, undoubtedly grinding into the rubber. A straight avenue loomed ahead, and I gave the Imperial all she had. The big limousine roared ahead, the massive engine picking up speed and quickly closing in on the blue compact. We were going downhill and at an intersection he cut over down another street, this one lined with cobblestones. It was a mistake for him. For both of us, in a way. In the chase, I hadn't seen the dead-end sign, as I'm certain he hadn't either.

I was closing in on him when I saw the massive building looming up ahead, low and wide. His headlights picked up the dead-end wall just beyond the building. He started to brake and saw the driveway to the right, just before the building. He tried for the turn, and I watched the light car spin on the cobblestones. He managed to get it out of the spin and turned his wheels for the driveway, but he wasn't going to make it.

He slammed sideways into the building. I tried to make the driveway but knew it was a lost cause as I spun the wheel. I felt the heavy car going out of control, the rear end pulling her into a hard skid but not hard enough. I was going to hit the corner of the building. I snapped off the ignition and, curling myself into a small bundle, cushioned my body against the back of the seat. The car hit the corner and I heard the entire front end go. I was bounced around but, outside of some bruises, I was unhurt. The car had barely stopped when I jammed a foot against the door and pressed. It pried open just enough to let me squeeze out.

The compact was empty, and I saw a door open into the building. The inside turned out to be a storage depot for the public buses. The cavernous floor, dimly lighted, held rows of green and yellow buses all neatly lined up against the walls. I heard shouts, then a shot—the .22 again. I saw the night watchman stagger out from between the rows of buses and collapse on the floor. I had Wilhelmina out and in hand and crouched over, I ran to the watchman. He'd been hit in the leg, but he was really more frightened than hurt.

"Back ... back there ... by the buses," he gasped at me, assuming I was a cop, though few cops wear tuxedos. He was an elderly man, grayhaired, florid-faced. I looked at the leg, tied a handkerchief around it to slow the bleeding and patted his arm.

"You'll be all right, Pop," I told him. "Just stay here until I can get you some help."

I moved off, still in a crouch, cautiously edging down the narrow space between the rows of buses. I kept Wilhelmina ready but I didn't want to use her. There was silence in the depot. I darted out from one row but I was seemingly alone. I advanced carefully, moving fast around each row of buses.

Suddenly I heard running footsteps. I pocketed Wilhelmina and took off in the direction of the sound. Then I saw the ramp at the rear of the depot, just wide enough for one bus and leading up to what was a second-floor storage or repair area. The ramp, dimly lighted, leveled off at the second floor. I was nearly two-thirds of the way up when I heard the heavy throb of a bus engine coming to life. The sound, in the cavernous building, bounced off the walls, echoing in all directions as I tried to pinpoint its exact location. As the engine shifted into gear I placed it, coming from the second floor. Then I saw the massive shape of the bus fill the top of the ramp and start down.

It took up the ramp from wall to concrete edge. I saw the driver gun the bus, heard the roar of the engine as he came down over the top of the ramp. I thought of firing at him but that wouldn't help me. The huge vehicle would continue its downward path. There was nothing to do but run. I started to race down, turning my head to see the huge dark bulk hurtling af-

ter me. It was strictly no chance. I'd
be flattened in seconds, crushed to a
pulp under that massive chassis. The
right of the ramp was a solid wall and
the left a two-foot-high ledge of concrete, more of a guide for the drivers
than a rail. I dived for it. My fingers
held for a moment, long enough for me
to swing my legs over and dangle from
the edge above the depot floor. If I let
go it would surely be two broken legs—
and a bullet in the head, no doubt.

I hung there, my fingers starting to
slip. The bus had roared by, but I
heard the screech of the huge tires as
the driver applied the brakes hard. He
skidded to a halt halfway down the
ramp. I heard him put the engine in
reverse. The bastard was going to back
up for another try. No, he wasn't, I realized instantly. He was going to back
up till he was even with me, open the
door and let me have it right between
the eyes. I was a sitting duck. Actually
a hanging duck. Listening to the heavy
bus backing up the ramp, I pulled myself up, every muscle howling in protest. I managed to throw one leg up

over the concrete ledge and I lay there a second. The bus was opposite me now. He braked, opened the door, but I had Wilhelmina out and I fired first.

The heavy Luger slug tore into him. I saw his body stiffen, half-twist in the driver's seat, and then the bus started down as he slumped forward over the wheel. The bus careened down the ramp, a huge green and yellow missile. I pulled my other leg up and lay there a second longer. By the time the bus reached the bottom of the ramp it was going at a fair clip. I watched it roll across the floor and slam into the buses parked on the opposite side. The metal-tearing, glass-breaking impact shook the building.

I put Wilhelmina back in her shoulder holster and walked down the ramp. Hurrying time was over for a while. The front of the bus had been pushed in and the man was wedged into the driver's seat, his head lolling lifelessly to one side. For the first time I got a real look at him. He was an Oriental, Vietnamese, I felt sure; he had the fine-boned frame of his people. I went through his pockets, not that I expected to find anything identifying him. Some loose change, a wallet with about ten bucks and in one pocket, the revolver. I'd been right, it was a Smith and Wesson .22 Kit Gun. I pocketed it and reached into his other pocket.

My fingers closed on a small metal object and I brought it out. I'd seen one before and I blew on it. It made no sound, at least not to my ears. It was a dog trainer's whistle, audible only to dogs, pitched at 10,000 cycles. Now, I asked myself, why the hell was this guy carrying a dog whistle? It was a bizarre note in what was fast becoming a very bizarre affair. That he was one of Sonyoung's men I had no doubt. Just what happened back at the senator's party was something else again.

I went over to the watchman, told him I'd call for medical help for him and then left. The Imperial was a battered, crumpled heap outside—a very long, expensive crumpled heap. I winced as I thought of Hawk's lecture. I caught a stray taxi a few blocks away and returned to the senator's house. It was swarming with police, and I had to use my identification to get back inside. Fillmore Benton's body had been taken away but the place was still exploding with photographers' flashbulbs. I found Senator Atkins still in the garden, ashen faced, talking to a police captain. The senator's eyes brightened when he saw me. I showed the captain my identification card and a glimmer of respect flickered in his otherwise expressionless eyes.

"Carter," the senator exclaimed. "Good God, you're back. Did you get him? Did you catch the killer?"

"I caught the man who escaped over the wall," I said. The police captain caught on immediately.

"What's that supposed to mean, cousin?" he said.

I grinned. "It means he wasn't the man who killed Fillmore Benton," I said. I pulled the Smith and Wesson from my pocket and handed it to the captain.

"This is all he was carrying," I said. "I think you'll find that the secretary was killed by something bigger than that."

"No doubt about it," the captain agreed at once. "We didn't look around for anything else. We figured the killer—the guy you were chasing— took his gun with him." He turned and ordered a search of the garden. It didn't take long. Bushes nearby offered up a .357 Magnum Colt. I saw Ferris Dickson at hand and Judy Howell. The cops had divided the guests up into small groups, and a detective was questioning each group separately.

"That's the murder weapon," I said, indicating the Magnum.

"The man you chased," the senator cut in. "He could have used that gun to kill the secretary, thrown it into the bushes and fled."

"Possible," I said. "But not probable. It's not logical for a killer to use one gun, throw it away and run off carrying another."

"Who says a killer has to act logically?" the captain asked. "I think the senator might have something. I think you caught the killer. Where is he?"

"Dead," I said. "He tried to take a bus without paying the fare."

I turned away. Let them think whatever they wanted to think. Someone else had shot Fillmore Benton, I was certain of it. But who—and, why? Ferris Dickson and Senator Atkins had been on the spot when I reached the scene. So had Judy Howell. Yet none of them saw anyone, according to their stories. A few other people were near enough to be there in moments, and they hadn't seen the killer flee. Had someone taken a shot at Senator Atkins, missed and hit Fillmore Benton? That held water for me. It was not only possible but in line with what we expected. Well, not exactly in line but it could fit.

The captain dismissed everyone. As Ferris Dickson passed me, the hard-eyed blonde still on his arm, he sneered, "Hardly my idea of protection, Carter."

He was gone before I could answer, which was probably just as well. But his words would come back to me and not merely because they rankled. I nodded to Judy Howell, turned and went inside to collect Linda. She was standing in a knot of Social Register friends, and we left at once.

As we drove back to my place, my mind was racing. There were new pieces to the puzzle, but they only served to complicate things even more. The Secretary of the Interior slain in the middle of a party at Senator Atkins' home. A fleeing Vietnamese whose gun hadn't done the killing. Then, what was he doing there? And why did he try so desperately to escape? And what the hell did the dog whistle in his pocket mean?

Maybe it didn't mean a goddamned thing, I told myself. Maybe he had a dog somewhere and used it for his dog. Maybe it was throwing me off the track and only confusing things unnecessarily. I decided to set aside the whistle as an extraneous bit and concentrate on more logical things.

Why would they want to kill the Secretary of the Interior? I had no answer for that one. Then why would they try to kill Senator Atkins, if they wanted him for their mind control experiments to get information. A dead mind is somewhat beyond control of any kind. It put a big hole in my theory that they'd tried to get the senator, missed and got Fillmore Benton instead. The whole damned affair grew crazier as it went on.

When I pulled up in front of my place, a chill, flat voice broke into my thoughts. "Take me to Cynthia's please," it said. Linda. I'd forgotten all about her. Now I glanced at her guiltily.

"Why Cynthia's?"

"First, you spent more time at the party talking to other people than you did me," she snapped. "Then you haven't said one word to me all the way over here. I prefer Cynthia tonight, thanks. At least she'll talk to me."

"I'm sorry, sweetie," I apologized. "Really I am. It just happens that way sometimes."

"I know, you've got things on your mind," she said, icicles dripping from every word. "And I'm not one of them."

"Now, Linda, doll—" I began, but she cut me off.

"Cynthia's, please," she said firmly.

I sighed. I wanted to tell her that I'd do better once we got upstairs, but I couldn't be that dishonest with Linda. My mind was whirling, racing, jumping from one thing to another. I knew it wouldn't stop, wouldn't turn off, not when it was going like this. I was disturbed, worried. Something was going on under our very noses, in the capital of the United States, and I couldn't get to the bottom of it. I put the car in gear and we drove to Cynthia's place in silence. I didn't blame Linda, though I had the fleeting suspicion that she was staying angry more as a matter of principle than anything else.

"Call me sometime, if you get interested in girls again," she threw at me as she stalked into Cynthia's apartment building. I had to grin after her disappearing back. I drove back to my place and went to bed. Sleep was something else again. Half the night went by as I tried to fit pieces together. All I came up with was a picture of the hand of the Vietcong or the North Vietnamese reaching across thousands of miles into the very heart of America's seat of government. The enemy was here, shadowy, sinister, combining a very ancient deviousness with a very modern knowledge of human behavior.

It was a chilling combination. We were sitting on a powder keg of unimagined proportions. Something big was going to blow, I was convinced of it. Maybe it was blowing already only we didn't know it and didn't understand it.

From my window, I could see the lighted dome of the capitol, white and beautiful in the night. It had stood supreme through many threats to its integrity, its meaning, its very spirit. This time, out of the shadows of Vietnam, from the sinister depths of one man's brain, it faced a different kind of threat, a threat to the mind of man which gave the nation it stood for the rights of life, liberty and the pursuit of happiness. If Sonyoung's mind control techniques made any headway, that white, graceful dome would govern a nation of human computers, programmed to act only at someone else's will.

I wasn't getting anywhere. I forced myself to go to sleep as dawn tinted the sky.

V

The next day, while the papers were filled with big black headlines about the murder of Fillmore Benton, and TV commentators were interviewing anybody and everybody who had been there, I met with Hawk for a few minutes. He made a face when I came into his office. He was just writing out a check for one nine-thousand-dollar limousine. His New England background always came to the fore at such times.

"Why is it your choice of vehicles is inevitably expensive, N3?" he asked, a little petulantly.

"I just grab whatever's handy, Chief," I said.

He held up his hand. "I know," he cut me off. "I've heard it before. It's even unfair of me to comment. You were doing your job and all that. It's always the same, and I'm sure it's true. But it always happens to be a Mercedes or a Jaguar or a limousine that's handy. I'm waiting for the day when a '39 Ford happens to be handy."

"I'll keep it in mind," I said. "Got anything new on Fillmore? What about the gun, any prints?"

"Nothing, and our investigation so far indicates he had no known enemies," Hawk said. "That rules out personal motives. There's always the stray psychopath, of course."

"They come right up and shoot people," I said. "They usually don't even run. This was a planned operation last night. Either the killer was there as one of the guests, or he was lying in wait with the character I chased."

"Ferris Dickson called to complain," Hawk said. "He said if we were expecting trouble, why hadn't we used greater precautions?"

"Yes, he made a crack about 'some protection' to me last night." I frowned.

"I told him we weren't expecting anything," Hawk said.

"I keep returning to those three weeks in Vietnam," I said. "The key is in there, I'm sure of it. We interrupted something. If I could find out exactly what, it might tell us what we want to know."

"I thought you were sure that Sonyoung planned to hold the senator to milk him of whatever vital information he had," Hawk said. "Weren't you afraid they were going to try another kidnap?"

"I still hold with that, Chief," I said. "But last night doesn't fit the pattern, I'll admit. It doesn't make sense, frankly. I'm going to have another crack at that girl, Judy Howell."

Hawk threw up his hands. "For God sakes, N3," he exclaimed, "you know she's a quick-tempered little scrapper. Be a little more subtle this time, will you? She's already plenty annoyed at you."

"Not any more," I said.

Hawk's noncommittal mask dropped over his face. "I might have guessed," he said. "Well, still take it easy. One day that special appeal of yours won't work."

"I'll quit then," I said grinning. I left him shaking his head. Sometimes I was sure he secretly approved my approach to women. Other times I felt his puritan background frowned at me. But I had an approach to Judy Howell in mind I hoped would work. It was simple. I was going to level with her—enough to get her cooperation, anyhow. And if she balked, then I'd take another look at her.

Judy wasn't at her office; I reached her at home.

"I stayed home because I felt sick all night," she told me over the phone.

"Too much joy juice last night?" I asked.

"Too much of Fillmore Benton's blown-apart face," she answered. "I couldn't get the sight of it out of my mind. I guess I'm not as tough as I thought. But I'm feeling all right now.

Is it time for that long talk?"

"It's time," I said, and she told me to come on up. I was at her door in half an hour, and found her in lounging pajamas, white silk with thin red piping around the edges, very smart and very becoming. As she led me into the apartment I watched her back move under the silk of the pajama top, looking for the slight telltale bulge made by the back of a bra. There was none, which meant that the breasts jutting out so vigorously were doing so unaided. Her little rear end bounced under the thin silken covering, deliciously appealing.

"What prompted you?" she said, turning and eyeing me, her brown eyes dancing.

"A remark you made," I answered. "You said I never let go and you're right. Not when I'm bothered, anyway, and I'm very bothered. Something very rotten is going on here. I can't tell you all that I know—you'll have to take my word for it."

"I'll take it," she said quickly, honestly.

"I'll make a bargain with you," I said. "You try to answer every question I ask you, as completely and as honestly as you can, and I'll promise to give you an exclusive on a story that'll make you the most sought-after correspondent in America."

She studied me speculatively, the brown eyes narrowed. "All right," she said finally. "You've got a deal. I'll do the very best I can. Start asking."

She sat down on a beige sofa and I took up a position next to her, turned to more or less face her.

"I want to know every little detail of what happened to you after the jet was forced down off Cam Pha," I said. "I don't want to hear the story you already gave. I believe every word of it. Or I believe *you* believe every word of it."

"What's that supposed to mean?"

"Nothing to you and a lot to me. Besides, I'm asking and you're answering, remember?"

Her eyes flashed for an instant, but then she relaxed and smiled.

"All right," she said. "I promise to try."

"What was the first thing that happened to you after you landed?"

"They marched us into the village and took us to the main hut . . . the place where you found us."

"What was the very next thing?" I asked.

"We were examined and minor wounds were treated. Then an officer —a colonel I think—came in and questioned us. I told you about that."

"Was there anything else that happened during that question period? You told us what he asked and stuff like that. Did anything else happen?"

"Someone brought him some tea and he gave us each a cup."

"You didn't say anything about that before."

"It wasn't important," she said. "A cup of tea?"

"We'll see about that," I answered. "What happened after the tea? Did you feel anything?"

"From tea? Of course not."

"Then what happened right afterwards?" I probed.

Her forehead wrinkled. "Right afterwards?" she repeated slowly.

"Right afterwards."

"I don't really know," she said. "I guess we just sat there a while and talked after he left."

"You guess?" I said sharply. Her hands were beginning to clench and unclench I noted.

"I don't remember anything *right afterwards*," she answered. "Not anything important anyway."

"Why not?" I shot out at her. "Why can't you remember what happened right afterwards? Did you talk long? Did you get up and walk around? Did you fall asleep?"

"I ... I don't *know*," she said, her face growing strained and her eyes flicking nervously toward me. "I didn't get up. I don't remember getting up anyway."

"Why are you so nervous?" I asked. "Look at you. You're all tensed up."

"I don't know why," she almost shouted at me. I saw her eyes suddenly filled with tears. She started to get up, but I put a hand on her arm and held her there.

"Why are you crying?" I asked.

"I don't know!" She was shouting

now. "Maybe it's a reaction to last night. I'm trying to answer your damned questions. I can't help it if I don't remember every little detail."

I put my hand on her shoulder. She was quivering, shaking. It was a funny reaction, one that I couldn't figure. It hadn't a damned thing to do with last night, I felt. She leaned forward and rested her head against my shoulder.

"I'm sorry," she said. "I don't know what's the matter with me."

"Let's start over," I said quietly. "What is the first thing you do remember after the cup of tea?"

She thought hard, her forehead wrinkling again.

"Standing naked in front of them," she said. "Being undressed by them. Then being pawed and slapped and threatened . . . all the things I told you about."

"Do you remember sleeping?"

"Sleeping?" she asked. "No . . . not actually, though of course we slept. I . . . I just don't remember exactly when."

"You can't remember any time when you slept?" I asked. "Did you sleep after you were subjected to an ordeal? In the night? During the day?"

"I . . . I don't remember exactly when we slept," she said, shaking her head. "Does anyone remember when they sleep?"

"Yes," I answered. "Friday night . . . when did you go to sleep? You remember, of course."

She was frowning at me, breathing rapidly.

"Friday night? I . . . I went to bed early," she said. "I was very tired."

"You see? You do remember, yet you can't recall anything about sleeping when you were held prisoner. Isn't that odd, to say the least?"

"I'm telling you the truth," she said, tears flooding into her eyes again. "I thought I remembered everything and I did, all the important things."

"Yes. You remember the beatings, the indignities, the thirst, the various ordeals you had to undergo."

"Aren't those the important things?" she asked.

"Maybe . . . and maybe not," I said. The lines from Sonyoung's manuscript were running through my mind: "A highly complex technique . . . the conscious mind is kept preoccupied while something else is happening in the subconscious mind."

I continued to question her. Her agitation would grow as I pressed her on some point, subside when I stopped probing. Finally, I was convinced that she didn't really know what had happened to her during her period of captivity. Neither, I felt sure, did Senator Atkins and Ferris Dickson. They *thought* certain things had happened to them, such as being deprived of water and nearly driven mad by thirst. There was no doubt in my mind that Sonyoung had at least started to apply his mind control techniques to them.

When I stopped questioning her, Judy put her head back against the couch and suddenly she was a very little girl, very unsure of herself and very appealing.

"You look like you could stand a drink," I said.

She nodded and pointed to a small cabinet. I fixed two rye and waters, plenty of rye and little water. She gulped it down fast and a rosy flush appeared on her cheeks. She nestled her head on my shoulder.

"Something's very wrong, isn't it?" she murmured. "And I'm part of it."

"Something's very wrong," I admitted. "But how much you're a part of it is another question."

"I'm suddenly very frightened, Nick," she said. "I don't know why, I just am."

She leaned against me, and I put an arm around her. The silk lounging pajamas were thin and the warmth of her body came through the fabric. I watched the steady rise and fall of her breasts beneath the silk, the nipples thrusting against the fabric. She quivered and lifted her face to look at me. Her arms began to circle my neck and I kissed her, savoring the soft sweetness of her lips. My hand brushed her breast and paused to rest there, now standing out straight beneath the pajama top. She moaned and her body twisted, and then she tore herself away and jumped to her feet.

"I . . . I shouldn't have," she said. "I'm sorry. It . . . something just came over me."

"And that's wrong?" I asked.

"No . . . not wrong," she said. "But that is my exclusive. I only give it to special people."

"And I'm not one of them obviously," I said, standing up.

She studied me, reflectively, her brown eyes wide and serious.

"Not yet," she said. "But you could be." She came over and put her hands on my chest. "Oh, God, you certainly could be," she murmured.

"What does it take?" I asked.

"A little more time, I guess," she said. "It means too much to me to hand it out casually."

I grinned down at her. "I'll be back." I said. "You may have helped more than you realize. Remember, this is strictly between us."

She nodded, and I leaned down and kissed her again. Her lips parted instantly and I felt her body tighten. She was a very desiring and a very desirable girl. There was a tinderbox quality to her. I wasn't ready to set a match to it, yet. But I wagered it would be a helluva bonfire when I did.

I swung the AXE staff car away from the curb and headed down Pennsylvania Avenue. Traffic was heavy and I drove slowly, trying to sort out what I'd learned from Judy Howell. Enough to make me wonder if I was really on the right track. Not about the Vietcong, nor about Sonyoung—they were the enemy all right. But I wondered about their real motives and objectives. I was still holding to my theory but now . . . I had to wonder.

I had driven down Pennsylvania Avenue, through the heavy traffic around Washington Circle and down New Hampshire Avenue without incident. I was almost back to my place when the small green car shot out of the side street at me. I saw it coming out of the corner of my eye, tried to turn the wheel, but there was really no place for me to go. It slammed into me broadside, not terribly hard but more than enough to push in the whole side of the car.

"Damn!" I said, slamming on the brake. I got out and came around to the other side, furious, to see a girl's head, hands held up to her face.

"Of all the stupid things to do," I said. "What the hell was the idea of that?" She dropped her hands and looked out the window at me, white-faced, terrified. She was pretty in a modest way. Brown hair, short, framed a round face. Blue eyes looked at me over a small upturned nose, lips pressed tightly together. My anger subsided a little, but only a little. She probably thought I was going to break her in half.

"Are you hurt?" I asked, relenting somewhat. She shook her head. I opened the door and she got out, swinging a pair of shapely legs around. She wore a brown, nubby suit and she was small-boned, neat, with small high breasts.

"It was my fault," she said apologetically. "I know it. I ... I'm sorry." She looked as if she were about to break into tears.

"Okay, okay," I said quickly.

"Don't cry about it. Take it easy."

"I don't know what happened," she said, blue eyes wide. "I just pressed on the accelerator suddenly. I don't know how I came to do it." Her eyes started to fill again and I managed to smile down at her.

"I believe you," I said. "Just relax. Nobody's hurt. Maybe a voice from space told you to step on the gas pedal. Or a mysterious message reached you. Maybe you're not really a girl. Maybe you're a mechanical robot, and you got your wires crossed."

I was trying to make a joke of it, to relax her, but she looked up at me suddenly wide-eyed. "Sonyoung," she said and started to turn away. I grabbed her arm.

"What did you say?" I asked quickly.

"Sonyoung," she repeated. "Professor Sonyoung. You sound just like him. He was a professor I had in college. He was always talking about how people could be made to do things like robots."

She was fishing in her purse. "I'll

give you my driver's license," she said. "I suppose your insurance company will contact me."

"Hold it," I said. "I want more than that. If you have dinner with me I'll forget about the damage."

She frowned up at me. "I'm very interested in this Professor Sonyoung," I explained. "I've been wanting to meet someone who was in one of his classes. How about it? Do I have a date?"

She smiled and the modest prettiness of her face grew quite attractive. "You're very handsome," she said. "I think any girl would like a date with you. And you'll forget about this?"

I nodded and gave her my most charming smile.

She gave a little laugh. "It's a deal," she said. "My name's Amy Dodd, and I've got to go home and change if I'm going out to dinner."

"Be off," I said. "I'll pick you up at eight sharp." She gave me her address and we parted. A stroke of luck, I said, congratulating myself. My car's smashed in side would be well worth it, if Amy came up with anything on Sonyoung.

I went home, changed and was at the modest brownstone of reconverted apartments at eight on the nose. Amy Dodd appeared in a little basic black dress that showed off her best feature, nice, smooth, well-shaped legs. Her little-girl breasts, small, round and high, nonetheless pushed themselves forward with a certain provocativeness.

Amy Dodd, I decided, was the kind of girl boys took home to mother. Certain boys, that is. She was essentially a small town girl in the big city, one of thousands who flocked to D.C. with high hopes. She was the kind who never really seems comfortable in the big town, the kind who never loses the screened porch, ice cream social look. I could have told her about herself and been right on the nose, but I let her talk over two Manhattans at the Embassy Club.

She had a mother and father back home in Ohio and a younger brother away at college. She'd been a home economics major at Claymoor, her first extended time away from home. No, she hadn't dated a great deal since leaving college. Amy Dodd was also frank and open, I learned. She'd never had a date with anyone like me, she admitted.

I got the definite idea that she wanted to make the most of it. We were midway into dinner when I brought up Sonyoung. I asked her if she knew about the morals charge.

"I was in his class at the time," she said. "I knew everyone involved. He was always bringing girls to his room and doing weird experiments with them."

"What kind of experiments?" I asked.

"Everybody was always very vague about them," she answered. "It seemed to be some kind of hypnosis, only they weren't really hypnotized."

"Did he ever have you up?"

Her eyes narrowed. "Yes," she said, in a defiant so-what tone. "Everybody went at one time or another."

"Did he ever try any of his experiments on you?"

"Maybe," she answered warily. "I don't really know if he did or not."

It was a strange answer, and I thought of Judy Howell. She didn't seem able to recall a lot of things either.

"He was really very nice," Amy Dodd continued. "I liked Professor Sonyoung. He was always very polite and mannerly. Some of the girls said he had them undress for him, but even then they said he was very proper about it."

I had to chuckle. "He was proper about being improper," I said.

"Well, I mean he was never rough or anything like that," Amy said. "He was always talking about being able to control people. He said he could make anyone do what he wanted them to do."

The mind control bit again. It was certainly plain that Sonyoung had perfected his methods and techniques with his students. That is, if, indeed, he had them really perfected.

Amy changed the subject abruptly, and after we finished dinner we went to a nightspot for a few more drinks. She clung to my arm as we talked, her eyes bright and shining. In between casual conversational bits, I tossed out questions about Sonyoung. Her answers always came unhesitatingly though never revealing anything terribly important.

"Did Professor Sonyoung ever talk about politics or world affairs to you?" I asked at one point.

"Not really," she said. "But he often told us that the average person did not deserve to have a mind, that most people couldn't think for themselves and would be better off if someone else did their thinking for them."

I smiled to myself. That fitted neatly into Marxist philosophy, replacing the sacredness of the individual with the omnipotence of the state. Amy had little else she could tell me about Sonyoung, and finally I relaxed and enjoyed myself watching her enjoy herself.

She was clinging even tighter to me

as we went back to her place. She asked me in for a nightcap. "I only have a bottle of Scotch," she said apologetically.

"Then it'll be Scotch," I said.

She lighted a small night light, just enough glow to let me see her in the small room. We finished the nightcap, and she came close and her arms went around my neck.

"It's been wonderful, Nick," she said, her eyes half-closed, her lips parted, the thin edge of her white teeth showing. "I don't want it to end."

I was a little surprised. It wasn't what I expected from Amy Dodd, small-town girl. But I had been fooled before by modest, proper "old fashioned" girls. Sometimes their desires are the most volatile, churning under a bottled-up facade.

I kissed her, long and hard, my tongue forcing her lips open, reaching into her mouth. She writhed in my arms but she didn't pull back. She would kiss me, tear her head away for an instant, then return to kiss me again. I rubbed my hand down her back, found the zipper of the little black dress and slowly pulled it down. I ran my hand down the skin of her back, down to the base of her spine where her small rear curved outwards.

"Oh, my God," she moaned. "Oh, my God." I pulled the dress forward off her shoulders, as she stood with eyes closed, body quivering, then off her breasts, letting the dress fall to the ground. She sat down on the sofa, eyes still closed, body still quivering. Her breasts were small, cupped in a half-bra I easily unsnapped. But they remained firmly in place and as my hand cupped one, she arched her back as though an electric shock had passed through her body.

Amy Dodd grabbed at my shoulders and clung to me, her eyes closed, her body writhing, her lips crushing against mine with a surprising savagery. Her desire was fierce and yet she seemed to be fighting some inner turmoil. As she turned to me, making gasping little sounds, her fists pounded against my chest, small, ineffectual little blows, as though they were trying to say something.

When I leaned down and kissed one of the small, high breasts, Amy gave a long, agonizing cry, something between ecstasy and protest. Now her hips were moving in circular, orgiastic motions and she was half-crying, half-moaning, her eyes closed. Amy Dodd was no experienced lover, but her feverish desire swept me along in a gathering intensity. It seemed as though all the pent-up emotions, the frustrated years, the small-town mores ripped apart in one frenetic crescendo.

As I began to really make love to her, tracing a line of ecstasy down her body with my tongue, her legs tossed in wild abandon, opening and closing, kicking out and drawing up as, once again, she seemed to want and to reject wanting at the same time. But now I was caught up with desire. I pressed myself down on her heaving body and as she slowly opened her thighs under me, I found her very essence.

Amy Dodd's closed eyes snapped open. For a moment there was a look of terror in them, and then she flung her arms around my neck and clung to me with an almost strangling grip. Her breaths came in long moans. She took a long time to reach the point of points, her moment of moments. When she did, she screamed a cry of rapture and terror combined. I'd never heard anything quite like it before.

I settled down with her on the sofa, holding her now still body against mine. When her harsh, shallow breathing finally grew normal, I pulled back slightly and saw twin lines of wetness, two streaks of tears on her cheeks. Women that cried at the time of their greatest rapture were not that uncommon, but in Amy's face I read sorrow, real sorrow. I started to move back but she pulled me to her.

"Stay here with me tonight," she breathed, eyes closed. "You must stay here with me."

Her head lolled against my shoulder. I shrugged, mentally. You're a strange little girl, Amy Dodd, I thought. But her round, soft breasts were nice to cup. I took one in my hand and settled back. Maybe she deserved this, I told myself. Maybe I had done a good deed tonight. I closed my eyes. I'd sleep for a while and then, later, when she had calmed down, I'd leave.

I dropped off to sleep, woke hearing a clock striking four. I felt Amy's breast slip out of my hand, felt her move from beside me quietly. I didn't move but watched her through slitted eyes. The hairs on the back of my neck and hands were standing up, I realized, the telltale sign of danger. It was a warning sign that had saved my life on more occasions than I liked to remember. But—danger? Here? With little Amy Dodd? I shook away the thought and watched her nymphlike figure move across the room, the little breasts standing up proudly. She disappeared into what I presumed was the bathroom.

It was the kitchen, and when she reappeared I caught the gleam of the long-bladed carving knife she held in her hand. She was tiptoeing toward me, the knife upraised. I let her come, my muscles tense, waiting. She stood above me, raised the knife higher and then struck. I shot out an arm, deflected the blow and grabbed her wrist. I twisted. She screamed in pain, and the knife fell to the floor. I kicked it aside and flung her onto the couch.

I was going to slam her across the face but I stopped, my hand raised. She sat there, looking up at me, eyes wide, mouth open, a dazed look on her face, as though she were seeing me for the first time. Then she began to scream. I slapped her. It stopped the screaming and she buried her face in her hands, her small, naked body quivering. As she touched her nakedness, she looked up, horror in her eyes, reached out and grabbed the little black dress and held it before her. I yanked it out of her hands. She tried to curl herself into a little ball.

"No, please . . . what are you doing?" she gasped. "Nick, stop this. Give me my dress."

"What am I doing?" I shouted at her. "You just tried to kill me and you ask me what I'm doing?"

Her head snapped up and I saw

pure horror flood into her face. "Oh, no," she gasped. "Oh, my God, no. No, I didn't."

"You sure as hell did!" I said. "There's the knife over there. Don't you remember?"

She was looking up at me, bewildered, eyes frantic, trying to remember. "I know I went into the kitchen," she said. "And I know I got the knife. But I don't know why."

I was watching her closely. She wasn't faking. Amy Dodd was quivering, shaking. Her eyes mirrored horror and fear and inner anguish. I tossed her the dress and she slipped into it instantly. She buried her face in her hands again and began to sob hysterically. I lifted her to her feet, roughly, my mind leaping back to when I'd first met her that afternoon.

"Why did you run into my car?" I demanded.

"I don't know," she sobbed. "I just had to, that's all."

"You remember my making love to you?" I asked.

"Oh, God, did you?" she said, sobbing. "I didn't know . . . I wasn't sure. I thought maybe I'd . . ."

"Dreamed it?" I finished for her. I asked her the next question, knowing the answer before I asked it.

"When did you see Sonyoung last?" I shook her for emphasis.

"Last night," she sobbed. "He came to see me. He said he had to talk to me."

"Why didn't you tell me that before?" I asked.

"I don't know why I didn't tell you," she sobbed. "I just didn't. He used to have me up three times a week at his room. He said I was one of his best subjects. After I left Claymoor, I finally managed to stop seeing him."

"What did you do last night when he came?"

"He brought some of his favorite tea with him, and we had tea," she said. "Then I remember listening to records. He finally left."

"That's all you remember?"

"Yes," she said. "I guess we talked in between."

I thought of my talk with Judy

Howell and how very alike her reactions had been, the fuzzy memory about certain ordinary things, the nervous agitation when questioned. I let Amy down onto the couch. She put her face into her hands again and sat quivering. I could put it together now. The bastard had set it up, right from the very moment of meeting. Whatever Sonyoung's methods, his mind control worked, I knew once and for all.

Amy Dodd had been turned into one of his computerized individuals. He had programmed her for certain responses and had gotten them. She had been programmed to smash into my car. I saw that damned manuscript before me, again "... a controlled mind, subject to a programmed response already determined by the controller." No doubt Amy Dodd had been mentally conditioned. From what she'd just said, he had worked on her for a long time and no doubt knew he could use her when he needed to. She was probably a good subject, as she said, just as some people are better subjects for hypnosis than others. The bastard had been diabolically clever, setting her up to drop his name, knowing it would make me bite.

"When did you need to get the knife to kill me, Amy?" I asked her. "What triggered you into it?"

"I don't know," she said. "But I remember hearing the clock strike four. Then I got up."

That had been it, the clock striking. He had programmed her mind to kill me when the clock struck four. Any signal would do to trigger the response, once it was firmly planted in the subject's subconscious. It explained a lot of things. Amy's strange, inner torment while making love, for one thing. He had undoubtedly programmed that in her mind, too . . . a desire on her part to have me make love to her. I decided to test it out. I sat down and pulled her around to me.

"We won't let this come between us, Amy," I said. I reached into the dress and grasped one of the small, firm breasts. Amy Dodd twisted away and leaped to her feet.

"No, Nick . . . I . . . I hardly know you, really," she said.

I was satisfied. That was the reaction I would normally have gotten from Amy Dodd. And here she had made wild, feverish love to me and she didn't remember doing so. It was, I realized, because it hadn't really been her making love. It had been her body but the mind belonged to Samuel Sonyoung. For a fleeting moment I wondered if I ought to send Sonyoung a note of thanks for a very unusual evening. I got up and gripped Amy by the shoulders.

"I want you to listen to me and do as I tell you," I said, looking deep into her eyes. "Sonyoung's an evil man. I think you're convinced of that now. He's involved in something evil, and he tried to use you in it. If he calls again, you're to hang up on him, understand? Can you promise me that?"

She nodded, wide-eyed. I was convinced she meant to do just that. I only wished I could know how deeply Sonyoung had controlled her mind. I stayed while she washed, got into a nightgown and robe, had a cup of coffee and seemed calmed down. When I left I was satisfied she'd be all right.

I walked down the steps of the brownstone and headed for my car. It was five o'clock in the morning and still dark. I was still thinking about Amy Dodd and the frightening import of what had taken place. I'd reached the car and was bending over to unlock the door when I caught the movement behind me. I whirled in time to take a blow alongside my head and to see that there were three of them. They tried to pin me against the side of the car but I dropped, grabbed one around the back of the knees and pulled.

He went over backwards and the rhythm of their initial attack was broken. From the crouching position, I dived forward over the fallen man, letting my shoes scrape over his face. His hat came off and a thick shock of black hair fell out from under it. These were more of Sonyoung's boys. Apparently the master had some misgivings about Amy properly carrying out his plans. These were insurance, in case I walked out alive. They were to correct that situation, but I had other ideas.

My dive had landed me up against an ash can. I picked it up, swung it in an arc and flung it at the other two who were coming after me. It caught one in the knees and he doubled over. I sent him down with a chop to the neck. The second one had leaped to one side off-balance, but he recovered quickly and now I saw a knife in his hand.

I'd had it for one night. First Amy, now this joker. A terrible anger welled up in me as the knife-wielder came at me, followed by another of the trio. I pulled Wilhelmina out and fired, once, twice, three times. The battle ended as abruptly as it had begun. I got in the car and drove off as windows opened and shouts for the police sounded. I drove home, angry, uncertain, knowing only that I didn't know a helluva lot more than when I'd set out that evening.

What I had learned was the chilling fact that mind control was not just a theory in an unfinished manuscript, but a practical, working weapon.

VI

Hawk had listened gravely to my story and, when I finished, leaned back and regarded me thoughtfully.

"They want to get rid of you," he said. "They must think you know something more than you do."

"I wish they were right," I said. "I thought I had their plans all figured out. Now I'm not so sure. I don't know what to think. Are they still after the senator, to program his mind? If that's so, why murder Fillmore Benton last night? And if that was an accident, if Senator Atkins was the intended victim, why kill him if they planned to use him?"

"Maybe we're off the track somewhere," Hawk suggested. "But there's an ideal set-up for them tonight. The Hotchkin Charity Ball at the Hilton."

I frowned. I knew the affair; it was an annual fixture of the Washington social scene, a costume ball.

"I take it I'm attending a costume party," I said.

Hawk nodded. "Better get a costume," he said. "And make it something light. No suits of armor."

"I'll be there," I said grimly.

I left, went to a local theater costume house and rented a matador's outfit, tight pants, three-cornered hat and cape. I called Judy Howell. I figured she'd be going, too, and I was right. We agreed to go together, and I picked her up at her place.

Judy was gowned as an Egyptian belly dancer. I say "gowned" using the word loosely. She wore bikini panties hung with spangles and baubles and a very brief bra trimmed with tinkling bells and baubles. A long, flowing, diaphanous veil completed the outfit. I watched as she moved across the room to fix us a drink and enjoyed the sight of her breasts, struggling to escape the confinement of the bikini bra. Judy Howell was quite a dish, I decided. She was one of those girls who seemed more beautiful each time you saw them. And that tinderbox was still very much there.

As she stood in front of me, letting me gaze down at the full swell of her breasts, the light in her brown eyes changed from an amused sparkle to a deep glow. I put down the drink, pulled her to me and kissed her. Her lips opened and her tongue circled in my mouth, eager, desiring. My hand moved across the top of her breasts, and I felt their softness reach out for more. She pulled away and she was breathing hard.

"Don't, Nick," she said. "We've got to go."

"I know," I said. "Aren't you thankful for it?"

She set her jaw and didn't answer, which was an answer of its own. We drove to the ball not saying much. Once inside the ballroom, we parted

company. Judy had her work to do
and I had mine. Hawk had given me a
description of Ferris Dickson's costume which he had asked the senator
for. It was a pirate. Perhaps fitting, I
thought. I spotted him now across the
main ballroom, the hard-eyed blonde
still his companion. The senator,
always a pillar of dignity, had skipped
the costume bit in favor of a tuxedo
and a black eye mask.

The place was packed with costumed revelers and keeping an eye on
the senator would be next to impossible. All I could do was hope for
the best. But I had planned for trouble
and this time there was no garden. The
party was contained in the main
ballroom, plus two smaller adjoining
rooms. Exit from the three rooms all
lead to the main lobby of the hotel, except for the fire exits, and each of
those had a uniformed fireman and a
policeman at them. Anybody fleeing
the scene would head out for the main
doorway.

I had a drink, took up a position
against the wall, standing at the best

place to view the ballroom. The senator was easy enough to spot, moving
through the costumed guests. There
were half-a-dozen pirates, and I kept
losing Dickson and having to pick him
out again each time. Judy was among
the crowd, and I spotted her occasion-
ally.

Things went perfectly normally,
and the hour grew late. I was beginning to think that Sonyoung and his
pals had skipped this one and began to
amuse myself, picking out the more
famous Washington figures. I saw E.
Miller Foster, Secretary of Agricul-
ture, and Gordon Green, a member of
the President's staff. I recognized
Henry Harlbut, Secretary of Defense,
and the junior senator from Virginia. I
gave up that game after a while and
began picking out the prettiest girls I
could find instead.

It was past one o'clock and the
crowd had thinned out a little when it
happened: another single shot that resounded through the ballroom. It
seemed to have come from one of the
corridors between the ballrooms, and I

didn't see Senator Atkins anywhere. Nor did I spot Ferris Dickson.

I saw Judy hurrying from the corridor as people started rushing toward it. I moved fast, staying close to the wall, circling the ballroom and getting to the exit in a matter of seconds. The shot had attracted others outside, including two cops who headed for the main ballroom. I had taken up a position in the lobby just before the revolving doors. I saw the figure struggle through the door to the main ballroom, pushing his way through the crowd blocking the doorway. He was costumed as a masked cowboy, and he spotted me instantly.

I hadn't any idea who had been shot. I'd decided that if something happened, I'd have to get the details later. I wanted the assailant this time. I started to move toward him, and he drew the gun from his western holster. The gun wasn't a cap pistol. I heard the glass of the revolving door shatter just behind me and I dropped to the floor.

He raced to one side and down a

flight of steps marked "Basement." I gave chase, pegging a shot at him as he disappeared down the stairs. I heard the running clatter as he continued on down to the sub-basement. Following, I saw the open door to the furnace room of the huge hotel.

As I entered another shot zinged into the steel door just above my head. I ducked behind a massive generator and started to move slowly along the wall. I saw a shadow and fired twice, but the wall was the only thing I hit. Then I saw him, wedged behind a heavy steel motor casing against the wall. To get at him I'd have to cross the only open area in the engine room. He'd bring me down before I took two steps.

He fired again, and the shot thudded into the wall just over my head. Suddenly I had an idea. Directly behind him, just over his head, a dozen pipes ran flush against the wall, horizontally. My Luger has a powerful, big-bore force to it. I took aim and fired. The bullet crashed into the pipe and a cascade of steaming, boiling water erupted from the hole. It shot out and down over him. He screamed in pain and raced out into the open. I drew a bead on him as he fell to the floor, holding his hands to his neck and head.

"Drop the gun," I yelled at him. "You're covered."

I didn't expect what happened next. I was ready for a possible wild shot fired at me, and I'd stayed behind the edge of the generator. Instead, he rolled across the floor, put the gun to his temple and fired. His body rolled once more and lay still.

I ran over to him. There's be no questioning him, I knew. I pulled the mask from his face. Like the other one, he was Vietnamese. Quickly, I went through his pockets. I frowned as my hand closed on a small metal object in his shirt pocket. I pulled it out and looked at it for a long moment. It was another dog whistle.

A lot of things suddenly exploded in my mind, a helluva lot of things. I raced up the stairway and into the ballroom, now packed with police as well as costumed dancers. I fought my way in toward the corridor where some space had been cleared. Once again I was relieved to see Senator Atkins standing there, but this time my relief was tinged with something else. I glanced around to see Ferris Dickson not far off. Judy Howell wasn't there, but I'd already seen her just after the shot.

The dead man was Henry Harlbut, the Secretary of Defense. One shot again, at near point-blank range, had torn his skull in two. I walked out, grim, angry and fearful, not for myself but for what might yet happen.

I walked along the street, head down, toward Hawk's home. It was a place I'd seldom visited. I knew the man liked his privacy, and he had a small house tucked away in the middle of the city. It was his refuge, his hiding place. I hated to do it but I had to wake him here and now. The things that had exploded in my mind were still exploding.

I fingered the dog training whistle in my pocket and I thought of the other one I had in a drawer at my place. I had dismissed it as "extraneous." I couldn't have been more wrong, I knew that now. I'd been wrong on a lot of things.

Hawk answered the door, wearing a smoking jacket. I was relieved to see he was still up. When he saw me he knew there was trouble, big trouble.

"I heard a news flash on the radio about the shooting, N3," he said. "They say a costumed man fled the ball and was cut down in a shooting match in the basement. That was your work, I take it."

"More or less," I said, and gave him a fast account of what had happened. When I finished he waited, reading the concern in my eyes.

"After Fillmore Benton was murdered . . . no, assassinated is the right word," I began, "Ferris Dickson made a crack to me about what lousy protection we had provided. It didn't do much to me then except irritate. But he was right, Chief. We've been protecting the wrong person."

Hawk's brow knitted. "Go on, Nick," he said.

"I know now why they've been after me so desperately," I said. "It wasn't what I knew they were afraid of, it was what I might figure out if I had enough time. And I've figured it out, Chief. We didn't interrupt anything when we rescued the senator and his party in North Vietnam. They had arranged it so we'd go in and bring them back. They supplied their troops with blank ammo so they'd fight and be slaughtered. They wanted to make sure we rescued their assassin—"

"Their *what*?" Hawk cut in, his eyebrows going up.

"Their assassin," I repeated. I was seeing that damned manuscript of Sonyoung's in my mind again. " 'The mind of man can be programmed to respond on command,' " I quoted from it. "It's true. Sonyoung has developed a mind control technique. Amy Dodd was proof of it. He has done the same thing with one of those three held captive in Vietnam."

Hawk was frowning as he listened. "Just think," I went on. "A person with easy access to every high official in the land, programmed to assassinate certain designated ones. Why, he'd be undetectable until it was too late. A human computer, programmed for assassination. Give him the predetermined signal and he acts. After he's done the deed, chances are he doesn't even remember it."

"That's a frightening supposition, Nick," Hawk said, gravely. "You're saying that Ferris Dickson or the girl, maybe even Senator Atkins himself, is an assassin . . . mind-controlled, programmed to kill on command."

"That's what I'm saying, Chief," I nodded. "And this time I know I'm right. Both Fillmore Benton and, tonight, the Secretary of Defense were slain from close at hand. And in both cases, all three of the possible suspects were at the scene."

"What about the Vietnamese you chased after the first killing, and the one tonight?"

"They merely gave the signal," I said. "With one of these. They each had one on them." I gave Hawk the dog whistle.

"But only dogs can hear this!" Hawk protested.

"When we find the assassin, we'll get the answer to that one," I said. "I don't have it now, but I'm certain it will explain itself then."

"It seems beyond belief," Hawk commented soberly.

Once more I recalled Sonyoung's manuscript. "Part of the technique is to fill the conscious mind with artificially produced stresses and anxieties," I said, "keep it occupied while the subconscious mind is being programmed. That's why they all said they were tortured by thirst but none of them actually was really thirsty."

"Where do we go from here, Nick?" Hawk asked. "I'd be in favor of picking up Sonyoung immediately."

"At once," I agreed. "The two assassinations so far were only dress rehearsals, Chief. They're after bigger game."

Hawk's eyes widened. "You mean—?"

I nodded. "Yes, the President. It wouldn't be hard—not for someone who can get close to him without suspicion."

"And that would take in all three of our suspects," Hawk grunted.

"Exactly," I said. "While you're having Sonyoung picked up, I'll bring in Amy Dodd for safekeeping. She might be of real help to us, if we can jog her subconscious mind enough to remember certain things."

Hawk grunted agreement and I left. I decided not to wake Amy at that unearthly hour but to get her first thing in the morning. I catnapped at my place for a few hours, then drove to Amy's apartment. There was no answer to my knock. She couldn't have gone to work yet; it was too early.

I went downstairs to the little two-car garage she shared with another tenant in the brownstone. Her car was there. I went back up, experiencing a sudden feeling of dread. Calling on memory, I took the edge of the celluloid covering for my identification card and slipped the lock on the door.

"Amy," I called. "Are you there?" And I walked in.

Amy Dodd was there, all right, but she wasn't answering. Her slender, naked body lay half off the bed. Her eyes were open, staring at the ceiling, and her throat trickled blood from a neat slash. She hadn't been dead too long. I felt her skin and it was still warm, still reluctant to grow cold. I looked at her again. Whoever had done it had his fun with her first. Or maybe it was more than one.

I felt a towering rage gripping me, tearing at my insides. It had been growing within me steadily. These bastards with their sophisticated excursions into mind control didn't turn away from old fashioned rape and torture. I pulled a sheet over Amy's lifeless young body and started out. On the way I spotted a button on the floor, a leather button from a man's jacket. Shoving it into my pocket I walked out into the morning and phoned Hawk from the nearest booth.

I knew what I'd hear but I wanted to hear it, anyway. Sonyoung had cleared out, slipped out through a side exit. He'd left in a hurry. I hung up and decided to play a hunch. If he'd left in a hurry, it was because he'd smelled that things were getting uncomfortably close. And if he'd left in a hurry, some of his friends might still think he was at home and visit him. I headed for his apartment, found the door unlatched and walked in. The loose manuscript had been taken but everything else seemed to be there. I sat down, paradoxically boiling with icy hatred of the man and all he stood for.

But I didn't figure him to have raped and murdered Amy Dodd. Oh, he might have given word to dispose of her, but he wasn't the kind to soil his own hands. I sat in the swivel chair behind the small table and waited. I'd been there maybe an hour, maybe a little more, when I heard the footsteps in the hallway, followed by a very discreet knock. I opened the door to see two Vietnamese standing there, eyes wide in surprise.

"Looking for somebody?" I asked. The taller of the two had a heavy jacket on with leather buttons. The top button was missing.

Something inside me exploded. I swung, putting all the hatred and fury inside me into the blow. It caught him on the jaw, and I heard the bone splinter. It lifted him off his feet and hurled him into the wall with such force the plaster cracked. I aimed a short chop at the other one, but he ducked and ran.

I didn't want any leftovers on this job. I picked the inert one up by the neck and gave him a karate chop on the side of the head. It would keep him quiet for the better part of the day. Then I lit out after the other one, reaching the front steps just in time to see him racing around the corner. I took off after him. He ran through the streets toward the waterfront, looking back fearfully at me following him. I didn't try to catch him. He was scared out of his wits and going someplace for protection. I wanted to see where.

He cut in behind a row of old, decrepit rooming houses, down a dark alleyway littered with broken gin bottles and empty beer cans. My rage hadn't dissipated with the one blow I'd landed on his friend. It had only been triggered, and now I was consumed with the desire to tear up the world. I saw the Vietnamese turn into the back door of the last of the rooming houses. I followed in after him.

There was a broken-down narrow wooden stairway plus four closed doors on the ground floor but finding him was no problem. I heard high-pitched excited chatter coming from the second-floor landing. There were other voices then, shouting in a cacophony of sound. I took the old stairs three at a time. At the top of the landing, the voices came from behind a closed door.

I hit the old door with my shoulder, slamming into it with full force. It flew right off the hinges into the room with me. I saw a table, chairs, cracked walls and Vietnamese ... six, eight, counting quickly. I knew where I was. These were Sonyoung's boys here in Washington, the ones who blew the whistles and tripped the horses and killed those Sonyoung wanted killed.

I caught the nearest one with a roundhouse right that sent him crashing into the wall. I didn't stop my forward motion but, whirling, slammed a second man with a left. As he doubled up I gave him a knee to the chin, and he fell like a log. The others, recovering from their surprise, came at me. I picked up a chair and broke it over the first two. They staggered and fell. With the jagged back of the chair still in my hands, I rammed another one in the face and listened to him scream as he clutched at his eyes.

One of them dived for my legs. I twisted away, shook him off and stomped down on his belly. He gasped in pain and clutched his groin. I heard more shouts in Vietnamese and the sound of running feet. There were more coming in. The place was loaded with them—the way it was loaded with cockroaches, no doubt. The more the merrier.

I upended the table, catching one of them with the edge as he rushed at me. As he half-fell over the thing, I brought a sledge hammer blow down on the back of his neck and he slid off, his larynx broken. I heard a shot and a slug hit the wall behind me. One of the newer arrivals had a gun. I dived behind the upended table and came up with Wilhelmina, firing fast and accurately. I sprayed the room, hearing my own curses as the bullets found their mark.

It was all over in a few minutes, and I stood alone among the broken, lifeless bodies. A few would recover, some only with bruises and minor injuries. But most of them were dead, and I felt the satisfaction of having cleaned out a nest of vermin.

I went out and phoned Hawk and the cops. Then I got my car and drove out to the Lincoln Memorial and stood before it, looking up at its solid, comforting bulk. He had fought so men wouldn't control the bodies of other men. He would have approved fighting to prevent men from controlling the minds of other men. Finally I walked away and got the car and drove back to my place. I had broken the back of the rank and file of the organization here in Washington. But Sonyoung was still loose and alive. The threat to the President was just as great as ever. Sonyoung didn't need his underlings for the ultimate coup. The programmed assassin was among us, already programmed to respond, unable to do anything *but* respond at the correct signal. I had the feeling I'd had not long before, of inexorable events coming to a climax, events which couldn't be stopped. The thought jarred me to my heels. *Could* the assassin be stopped? It was a frightening question, and I tossed it at Hawk the next day.

"Suppose it comes down to the wire, Chief?" I asked. "What do we do?"

"It's coming down to the wire, N3," he answered. "On Monday the President is going to officially open the new shipyards on Chesapeake Bay. Everybody will be there. He'll make a speech. There'll be distinguished visitors, the whole bit. It's going to take place inside the new indoor drydock building. Chairs and a speaker's platform have been set up."

"Monday," I said, turning it over in my mind. "That gives me two days to get a lead. I doubt if I could get one in two months."

"Then let's take your question, Nick. Make believe it's Monday. What do we do?"

"We could see to it that Senator Atkins, Ferris Dickson and Judy Howell don't attend the ceremony," I ventured, knowing as I said it that it just couldn't work that way.

"How, N3?" Hawk said, eyes gray steel. "By telling them we think one of them is a programmed assassin? First of all we have no proof to support such an accusation. Secondly, they insist on being there and nothing happens? Can you imagine where we'd be then? Crucified, that's where we'd be."

Hawk's hypothesis had raised an

angle I hadn't considered. Sonyoung was just clever enough to let his programmed assassin attend and not give him the signal. Then my name would be mud but, more importantly, his man would be free to strike at another time. But I had to go on the conviction that Sonyoung intended to strike, to kill the President of the United States via his controlled assassin. When that happened, he could write his own ticket in many parts of the world. There were many waiting for a weapon such as mind control. All those who believe that the end, not the means, is all that matters.

"Any chance of breaking the assassin down into admitting he—or she —is the one?" Hawk threw out.

"None whatever, Chief," I told him. "Because he doesn't know himself what he is and what he's doing. It's an act he commits entirely outside and apart from his real self. The only way to break the spell, if you want to call it that, is to do what I did with Amy Dodd—stop him in the act. Then the whole process shatters. But once one of the Sonyoung's computers commits whatever he's been programmed for, he reverts to his normal conscious self."

"Then I suggest you figure out what we can do on Monday, or it will be a black day for America and for the world."

"Sure thing," I said. "Nothing to it."

I walked out, angry and frustrated and feeling very helpless. Once Monday came and the President of the United States was in that shipyard, on that speaker's platform, Sonyoung held the trump cards—unless I identified the programmed assassin first, or somehow got to him before he or she got to the President.

I had to try to sound out the three suspects, try for some little lead that might help me. I had nothing to lose anymore. Now it was a race, a three-cornered race with time and death in the other two corners. With each tick of a second, the odds mounted astronomically. But I was going to be in there fighting till that very last second. I gave myself through Sunday night to come up with a lead. If I had none by then, all my attention was going to zero in on that shipyard.

Sonyoung would be in there somewhere, I knew. He had to blow the whistle . . . the trigger mechanism, the signal to set off the programmed human computer. Somehow, I had to blow the whistle on Sonyoung first.

VII

I showed up at Judy's Saturday morning, and she was surprised to see me. She had just finished her shower and had a loose terry cloth robe wrapped around her. Its salmon color put a soft glow into her cheeks.

"The President is dedicating the new Chesapeake Bay shipyard Monday," I said casually. "Are you going to be there?"

"Why, yes, as a matter of fact, I am," she said. "Why? Are you going too?"

"Maybe," I said, a sinking feeling inside of me. I had hoped Judy would say no, she wouldn't be there.

"How come you're going?" I asked, still trying to keep my voice casual. "I wouldn't guess that to be an item for a woman's magazine."

"You're right," she said. "It wouldn't be normally. But I'm still doing that series on Senator Atkins, remember? Living every moment of his official day with him from the woman's angle."

Neat, I told myself. Neat and reasonable and perfectly in order. I saw her in my mind walking from the corridor of the Hilton seconds after the shot that killed the Secretary of Defense was fired. It was a picture I didn't want to recall and the thought that went with it was even more disturbing. I looked at Judy, at her fresh, very American kind of good looks, at the loveliness of her rising bust under the robe. My hands clenched involuntarily in anger as I thought of Sonyoung. Thanks to him, this luscious creature could be an assassin.

"What's the matter, Nick?" she asked suddenly. I had forgotten how perceptive she could be. "You were looking at me as if I were something from another world, something you'd never seen before."

I passed it off with a laugh, but she was so right. I had been seeing her for a moment as a killer, not as the warm, desirable creature I knew.

She came up and stood before me. The robe parted just enough to let me see the beautiful, tantalizing curve of her breasts. Dammit to hell, I told myself, if it was Judy I'd find out in time and I'd be sick about it . . . then. Right now she was an eminently desirable girl.

I grabbed her and kissed her, parting her lips with my tongue. My hand slipped inside the robe, and the tinderbox almost burst into flame.

She gasped and grabbed my arm, holding my hand tight against her breast. "Oh, Nick . . ." she half-moaned. "Oh, . . . Nick, Nick."

I wanted to move my hand but she was holding it in a viselike grip. I freed a thumb and rubbed it across her nipple, flat and smooth. She gave a cry and twisted away from me, pulling the robe tight.

"You'd better go, Nick," she said, her voice trembling. "Or wait outside until I get dressed. You're too dangerous to have around this way."

"If it's that bad what are you waiting for?" I asked. "Why don't you be honest with yourself?"

"I have my reasons," she said, her pretty jaw set firmly, the way I'd first seen her on the C-47 after the rescue.

"What were you doing coming out of the corridor a second after Henry Harlbut was shot?" I flung at her, watching her intently.

She turned to face me, eyes blazing. "I was just on my way to the main ballroom when the shot rang out."

"Most people turn around when there's a shot behind them," I said.

"Not me anymore," she said heatedly. "Not since I saw Fillmore Benton's blown apart face. I don't want to see another one. I just made myself keep walking."

Another perfectly plausible explanation that told me nothing. I couldn't fault it. I could only go on wondering.

"I think you'd better leave," she said icily.

I went downstairs a little ashamed of myself, yet knowing that Judy Howell was as good a candidate for the assassin as any of the others. I drove off having to face the fact that perhaps she was the star suspect. Apparently Sonyoung had found the feminine mind easier to work with because most of his experiments had been with girls.

I stepped on the gas and headed for Senator Atkins' home in Bethesda. The butler ushered me in, and I found the senator in a warmly furnished study, looking very tired and depressed.

"Still probing, Carter?" he said, trying to smile. "You fellows never let up, do you? But then I suppose that's what makes you what you are."

"You look very tired, Senator," I said. I almost added "and depressed," but I thought it might be rude. As it turned out, he said it himself.

"I'm more than tired, Carter," he

said. "I'm depressed. Harlbut's death upset me terribly. Fillmore's was tragedy enough and to be followed so soon by another—? What's happening in the world, Carter? You fellows get around. Are we all going mad?"

"Maybe," I said. "Maybe. Anything else bothering you, Senator?"

"I can't sleep," he said. "I toss and turn. I feel as though I'm living under some terrible cloud. My family complains I'm not at all with it, and they're right. The doctors say it's just nervous tension. God knows my job will give it to you."

I agreed with him and we talked some more. I probed cautiously, but nothing came out of the meeting. There were a lot of things I could seize and run with, if I let my imagination take off. But there was no more time for imaginative theories. Unless I got hold of hard facts, worthwhile facts, I couldn't move against any of them, and all I had so far were more straws in the wind.

It was dark when I returned to Washington and I decided to leave

Ferris Dickson for the next morning, Sunday. He lived with a brother in a private house on the outskirts of the city. I'd never met the brother, but research told me he worked as a television producer—when he worked.

Ferris opened the door. When he saw me, he glared.

"What the hell are you doing here?" he growled. The boy wonder had a morning stubble and looked thoroughly disagreeable. He also smelled of liquor.

"I want to talk to you," I said. "May I come in?"

"No," he snarled. "You've got a helluva nerve coming here."

"I'll make this an official visit if you like," I said calmly. "Then you'll have to talk to me."

He opened the door. A nasty smile twisted his lips. "All right, Carter," he said. "Come in. I'll see that your visit is made interesting for you."

I walked into a richly furnished living room, spacious and decorated with modern prints that contrasted with bearskin throw rugs and ornamented lamps. He went over to a home bar, poured himself a drink and didn't offer me one, pointedly. His normal haughtiness had been replaced by a truculence. Now he looked at me and gave a snort.

"You coming here." He laughed. "That's rich. Why are you trying to ruin my career, Carter?"

The complete unexpectedness of the question surprised me, and my face showed it.

"Don't give me that look," Dickson said. "I know your kind—nasty, petty little characters who envy anyone who's making it big."

"How am I trying to ruin your career?" I asked, in honest bewilderment.

"By giving truth serum tests. That gets around. It makes people think you're a liar."

"Nonsense, Dickson," I said crisply. "You were all given sodium pentothal—the senator, Judy Howell and you. No one was singled out."

"You need a lesson in humility, Carter," he said, downing his drink.

He was determined to pick a fight. I'd seen it before, many times. Whatever you said, it was wrong. But I had to try.

"I didn't come to argue, Dickson," I said patiently. "I just wanted to get some thoughts from you."

"You've got my thoughts, Carter," he said. "I'm going to give *you* something to think about before you throw any more rocks at my career."

He seemed unusually belligerent. Even liquor wouldn't make him so rash. I learned the answer soon enough. "Fred!" he called out suddenly at the top of his voice. "In here, Fred!"

I heard footsteps coming down a stairway someplace and Fred appeared, wearing only gym tights and carrying a barbell in each hand. Muscles bulged all over Fred, the kind of muscles that come only from weightlifting and body-building exercises.

"This is the character I told you about, Fred," Dickson said. "My brother and I are going to give you a working over, Carter."

Fred Dickson bore only a slight facial resemblance to his brother but shared with him weakness of character. Ferris Dickson disguised his with snobbish arrogance; Fred Dickson, with his muscles. But it was there. I'd seen it in muscled bully boys before. They were dangerous, usually basically sadistic, but if you knew what to do the weakness would show itself. Fred Dickson smiled, a mean smile.

"I take care of guys who pick on my kid brother," he said.

I said nothing, but I was wondering why Ferris Dickson was so determined to give me a going over. Was his career really floundering and did he need someone to blame, someone to make the scapegoat for what were his own mistakes? Or was there something more? Was he seizing an unexpected opportunity to prevent me from showing up tomorrow at the dedication?

Whatever the reason, I knew I'd walked into trouble. Muscle-boy Fred would be more than enough to handle without brother Ferris to distract me.

I decided the first thing to do was to take Ferris Dickson out of the picture. It would have to be vicious, fast and complete.

"I don't want this," I said again. "I just came by to talk to you."

"We do want it," Ferris Dickson said nastily.

I shrugged, half-turned away from him to look at Fred who stood still holding the barbells, loosening up his arm muscles. I stood quietly for half a second and then, spinning on my left foot, I sank my fist into Ferris Dickson's gut. It went in almost to his backbone. His eyes popped as he doubled over. He tried to scream, but no sound came out. He pitched forward, holding both hands to his midsection, drawing his knees up and writhing on the floor, his face contorted in pain. He wouldn't be getting up for quite a while, more than enough time for me to take care of Fred . . . or vice-versa.

The suddenness of my move had taken Ferris Dickson completely by surprise and had infuriated his big brother. I was ready for Fred Dickson's charge, but now it was his turn to come up with a surprise. Instead of charging, as I expected, he flung the two barbells at me. I was able to dodge one, but they came almost simultaneously and the second one caught me on top of the forehead.

My head exploded, and the room was whirling. I saw three or four Fred Dicksons rushing at me, then his powerful arms grabbed my legs. He was lifting me, tossing me through the air. I hit the long sofa at the side of the room, bounced off it and onto the floor. Luckily, instead of cracking my skull again on the floor, I landed on one of the bearskin throw rugs.

The room was still spinning but not as much. I rolled over as Fred Dickson grabbed for me. A heavy hand fastened onto my shoulder, and he pulled me back. I drew up my knees and pushed, shoving him off balance as he tried to come down on me. My head was starting to clear when he got hold of my right leg and twisted.

Rockets of shooting pain went up

my spine and I had to come around
with the pressure. He had me in a viselike grip again, and now I lifted and
swung like a sack of wheat. This time
I went flying into the bar cabinet, and
my head hit the edge of the wood re-
soundingly. Once again I saw stars,
heard the crash of glasses and bottles.

A water pitcher atop the bar toppled, dousing me with ice water. It
couldn't have come at a better time.
My head cleared enough to see
Muscles rushing at me again but this
time I dived down, hitting the floor as
his powerful arm swept over me. I
grabbed one of his oaklike legs and
yanked on it. It upended him, and he
crashed backwards, arms flailing out
for me.

I didn't want close quarters with the
powerful sonofabitch. I rolled away
and was on my feet while he was still
on his hands and knees. I aimed a kick
at his jaw but he was surprisingly fast.
One huge hand grabbed my ankle and
yanked. I hit the floor flat on my back,
and he dived for me. But this time no
barbell or cabinet had clouded my

head. I met his dive with my foot and heard him grunt as the foot hit his chest.

He toppled off to one side and I was on my feet again. He got up, a thin, anticipatory smile on his face. This time he came in swinging, huge, roundhouse swings, powerful but Muscle-bound and slow. I parried them easily and gave him two light jabs. He tried a tremendous right hook which I avoided and countered with a light left.

His smile grew broader and the glint in his eyes grew brighter. The weakness of my blows was giving him reckless confidence. Good, you thick-skulled bastard, I thought. He came in swinging, confident I was a pushover. I knew better than to waste punches on that highly developed ironlike midsection. I avoided his swings, circling to the right. He was sure I was easy, a nothing. All he had to do was connect with one good blow. And I was sure of the inherent weakness under all that muscle.

He paused to set himself, lowering

his arms for an instant to loosen the overdeveloped trapezius muscles. I went into action. My first hard punch was a beautiful right, delivered in a straight line with everything I had in it. It crashed into his mouth and blood spurted out from between his lips. I almost laughed at the look of utter shock and surprise that flashed across his face. It didn't stay there long, because I followed the right with a cluster of punches.

I sent them in from all angles, hard and fast, hooks, jabs and right and left crosses. A particularly sharp left hook opened a gash over his right eye and more blood ran. My estimate was right. The muscles were a disguise of a kind. There were no guts to back them up. When Fred Dickson was hurt as he was now, when his body-beautiful face was taking punishment as it was now, he cringed and tried to protect himself with his huge arms. There was no fighting back, only a childlike effort to avoid further pain.

I gave him a tremendous right to the

ribs. He brought down his arm to protect himself, pain and I let him have another whistling left that shredded the already gashed eyebrow. He went backwards over a chair and hit the floor.

"Oh, God . . . My face! My nose!" he screamed, seeing the blood covering his hands. He stumbled to his feet not even glancing my way, and raced for the bathroom, whimpering. I heard the sound of tapwater being run furiously. Ferris Dickson was still curled on the floor, holding his stomach, breathing heavily in pain but his eyes were open and looking fearfully up at me. I stepped over him and walked out. Outside, I took a deep breath and got in the car.

I drove back to my place, driving slowly, wondering about what I'd learned these last two days. Nothing to help me for what lay ahead. In fact, I'd learned things which only made matters worse. I'd wanted to eliminate at least one, hopefully two, of the suspects, draw some kind of picture that would let me concentrate on only one of them. Just the opposite had happened.

Senator Atkins couldn't sleep nights. He felt as if he were "living under some terrible cloud." That might mean simply ordinary tension brought on by his work and events. Or it could mean a lot more. Sonyoung's manuscript referred to the "normal resistance of the mind to control." If the mind normally resisted control by an outside source. Sonyoung's techniques might set up a terrible inner conflict with the mind fighting against superimposed responses. That could well explain Senator Atkins' vague, undefined feeling of "living under some terrible cloud."

Judy Howell had pat, reasonable explanations for every unusual action. Maybe when I saw her walking away from the corridor seconds after the shooting at the ball, she had forced herself not to turn. Maybe. And maybe not.

Ferris Dickson was determined to have me beaten to a pulp. Personal resentment only? Or something more? Could he be reacting to subconscious influences, somehow knowing I was the threat to the successful completion of his programmed response?

I had no answers. I only knew one thing: that I hadn't been able to eliminate any of them. That, in fact, each of them had exhibited things that made him a more likely candidate. I looked at my watch and thought of the day that would dawn in but a few short hours.

It wouldn't be enough to just sit there, waiting and watching to see which of the three rose to assassinate the President of the United States. It would be too late then. Things would happen too fast to be stopped. I needed some way to get the jump on the assassin, to be alerted to the moment of death, to know the moment he knew. Seconds would be vital. Half-seconds could spell the difference. But how? Was there a way? Or was that feeling I had of inexorable events marching to an inevitable close doomed to come true?

Hawk called me and wasn't surprised at my having unearthed nothing. He hadn't any answers either.

"I thought of having only one entrance and screening everyone who came through," he said. "But it wouldn't work. First, he'll probably be in disguise. Second, the new shipyard has been going for months—this is only the official dedication. He could be inside somewhere, hiding, waiting, right now."

I agreed and then wrestled with his next thought:

"Suppose we have the dedication called off, N3?" he said. "Then there'd be no chance of an assassination."

"Until next time," I said. "And maybe then we'd be even less prepared. We'd be sitting, wondering when the bastard was going to set his human robot into action."

"You're right, N3," Hawk said, reluctantly. "We've got to go with it tomorrow. But if the President is assassinated, we'll be crucified. One hundred and ninety million people will be second-guessing us. We, in short, are sitting on a powder keg, N3."

He hung up. There wasn't anything more to say, anyway. We were sitting on a powder keg, and there was no question that it would go off. Somehow, I had to cap the explosion.

I poured a snifter of my best brandy and sat down on the sofa. *Think, damn you,* I told myself. *Think like you've never thought before.* It was ironic. I'd thought my way and fought my way out of hellish spots in every corner of the world, and here I was at home . . . so goddamned helpless.

VIII

The Chesapeake Bay Shipyards had
been open for nearly three months.
The official dedication that had been
delayed for one reason and another
was taking place inside the latest piece
of shipyard construction: a huge,
enclosed air-conditioned drydock
where a vessel could be repaired faster
than anywhere else in the world.

The rest of the yard had been put to
working use but the enclosed drydock
had been left unused, awaiting the official dedication. Rows of folding
chairs now filled the cavernous building, standing on thick metal plates

that had been laid to cover the wide deep tracks used to pull vessels up into the great indoor basin. Most of official Washington was already seated on the raised speaker's section and the audience jammed the seats, flowed out to stand along the walls.

The shipyard had been a major effort for the American shipping industry, supported by a combined banking, management and labor union coalition. The resulting ticket distribution assured an overflow crowd. The yard was officially closed for the day, and the crowd was channeled into the dedication area, avoiding the clutter and disorder of a working shipyard: the long ladders leaning against the frames of vessels taking shape, the piles of lumber and planking, the ropes and paint cans and scaffolds and all the other working paraphernalia.

The President, who would sit directly behind the speaker's lectern, had not yet arrived as the audience listened to preliminary speakers. Ferris Dickson sat across the narrow aisle from the empty seats that the President and his party would occupy. Senator Atkins was sitting a few rows behind the President's chair. Judy Howell had a seat three rows further front than Ferris Dickson but perhaps the best one for observing the President.

The man with the dog approached the entrance gate, produced a ticket for the speaker's platform seats and was ushered through solicitously. The powerful German shepherd walked ahead of the man, held back by the triangular metal handle and harness of the Seeing Eye dog. The man adjusted his dark glasses and secured his thin, white cane over his arm as he followed the dog, taking short, cautious steps.

Anyone watching closely would have seen that the dog really didn't seem to be leading the blind man too well, walking more at his side than in the lead as he was supposed to do. An observant person might also have noticed that the shepherd was a helluva lot bigger and more powerful than the usual Seeing-Eye dog. But nobody was watching that closely and that was fine with me. The set-up was the best I could put together in such a short time. The dark glasses hid my eyes and the German shepherd was no Seeing-Eye dog but a trained attack dog I'd borrowed from Army K-9 Training Center in Bethesda.

An usher showed me down an aisle to my seat, the only one still unoccupied, about three rows back of the rows where Judy Howell, Dickson and Senator Atkins sat. The woman in the next chair shifted her glance. The blind man's dog lay down at his side, quietly. The woman, a somewhat overdressed, matronly type, spoke to her gentleman companion, and they both leaned forward to look at the shepherd and smiled in satisfied approval.

"Marvelous dogs," I heard the woman say. "So intelligent and gentle." She was right, of course, about the Seeing-Eye dog. This shepherd was intelligent but "gentle" was not quite the word for him. He was, I prayed, my four-footed ace-in-the-hole. I'd had Dickson, Judy and the Senator spotted from behind my dark glasses but I wasn't going to try to keep my eyes jumping from one to the other of them. More important, I needed those split-seconds. I needed to know the instant the assassin received his or her signal to act. Anything less would be fatal.

I heard the roar start at the back of the building, behind where we sat, heralding the arrival of the President. Shouting and applause accompanied his trip down the aisle beside me. Those around me stood up and I did too. The big German shepherd got to his feet and I felt tense. I stroked his neck with my hand, soothingly. Major Dennfer at the K-9 Center had given me instructions as to what to do when the time came.

I watched the President take his seat only three rows ahead of me and then sat down with the others. The clubwoman next to me held my chair to keep it from moving as I sat down, and I gave her a brief smile and a murmured thank you. I shot a glance

at my three candidates for murderer.
They were taking their seats again
with Judy Howell a little slower than
the others, casting a longer look back
at the President.

The President was introduced and
began his speech. Every eye was on
him, every ear tuned to his words . . .
except mine. I was looking down at my
faithful Seeing-Eye dog. As the President spoke, I never took my eyes off
the powerful shepherd. He lay at my
side, unmoving, head cradled on his
forelegs stretched out before him. The
President's words were just mean-
ingless sounds droning on to me.

The palms of my hands were wet
with perspiration, and I wiped them
on my pants. The President had
spoken for nearly fifteen minutes, and
I realized he must be nearing the close
of what was scheduled as a relatively
brief dedication speech. I kept my
eyes on the shepherd, and then, suddenly, I saw his ears snap up to alert.
His head came up and he sprang to his
feet, listening. He had heard the whistle, the whistle which only he and one

other living thing in that arena could hear, the signal that would turn one of three people on that speaker's platform into a programmed assassin.

I looked away from the dog, scanned the rows of seats ahead of me. A figure rose, moving with sure, determined swiftness, silver hair glistening under the lights. Senator Atkins started toward the lectern and the President of the United States.

The blind man jumped to his feet, tore off the dark glasses, unbuckled the dog's harness and, pointing to the figure striding toward the lectern, gave the command to attack. I got a glimpse of the woman beside me, her mouth hanging open and her eyes round as saucers as she watched the blind man. The shepherd covered the few feet distance in three leaping strides, just as the senator drew a .357 Magnum Colt from inside his jacket pocket. Trained for this very kind of situation, the shepherd leaped, sank gleaming, white fangs into the senator's gun arm. The shot resounded in the huge area, but the bullet went harmlessly into the floor as the dog pulled the arm down. Retaining his grip, the big shepherd shook and pulled with his powerful neck muscles, and Senator Atkins fell forward on his knees.

All hell broke loose. The Secret Service men went into instant action, some of them forming a human shield around the President, others rushing to seize the senator and disarm him. I yelled the release command at the K-9 dog and, with a growl of reluctance, he loosened his grip. A red stain immediately spread over the senator's sleeve. I had time to see him pulled to his feet, his face ashen, strained, horror in his eyes—the same look of incredulous disbelief I'd seen on Amy Dodd's face. Awareness of what he had almost done was flooding over him. Stopped in the very act, the control mechanism had aborted and the mind erupted in an explosion of recall and realization previously denied it.

I had gambled—and the gamble had paid off. Had I and the assassin not "heard" the signal to kill at the same time, he would have had those few seconds jump on me—and those few seconds would have meant death for the President of the United States.

At first stunned and aghast, the crowd was now beginning to rumble with excitement, watching the life-and-death drama going on before their very eyes. Hawk, I knew, was somewhere in the vicinity, and the Secret Service had things under control already. I turned and raced up the aisle for the exit. Everything that had happened, everything we had managed to prevent would all go for nothing if Sonyoung escaped us. He'd find another mind to control, another human being to program for assassination.

Outside, I ran around to the side of the big drydock where I'd seen three small side exit doors. The last one, at the farthest end, opened, and Sonyoung came out. He looked around, moving cautiously, and he spotted me.

He began to run, not fast, but in springy, ground-consuming steps, vaulting over lumber and crates with ease. I took after him, dodging and hurdling wooden horses, ladders and crates. Sonyoung was racing between the hulls of two freighters under out-of-water repair and painting.

He disappeared from sight as he ducked under the huge propeller of one of the ships and was lost amid a welter of ladders and ropes and sheets of metal standing on edge against the giant hulls. I cursed silently and ducked under the propeller in pursuit. I halted, listening for the sound of his running footsteps, but I heard nothing.

I drew Wilhelmina and moved forward carefully. The wily bastard wasn't running. He was in here someplace, trying to hide. I saw a long, twenty-five-foot ladder leading up to an open side hatch in the hull of one vessel. If he'd gone up there he'd be there a while, and I could go after him. First, I wanted to finish searching the area around the two hulls. I moved carefully, the Luger ready, peering behind each upright steel plate.

I never heard the huge ladder start to come down on top of me. Suddenly I had a feeling of impending danger.

Perhaps I did literally feel it, a sudden change in the air as the huge ladder started to fall. In any case, I spun around and saw it coming down on me, all twenty-five feet of it. Through an opening between rungs I glimpsed Sonyoung standing in the open side hatch, smiling that controlled, sly smile.

Between the two hulls where I was there was little room to maneuver. I tried to dodge sideways, but I was too late. I hunched up my shoulders, tightening every muscle, twisting to take the force of the impact on my arms and side.

The ladder was not only long but damned heavy. It hit me with shattering force. Pain shot up my body, a numbing agony, and I fell heavily, the ladder on top of me. Twisting my head, I saw Sonyoung swinging down from the open side hatch on a rope and then a gray semi-darkness curtained my eyes.

Blinded by that gray, flickering world, I felt a heavy weight being lifted from me as Sonyoung moved the ladder. I tried to move, to clear my head, but the numbness still gripped me. I felt Sonyoung take Wilhelmina from me, and then I was being dragged across the ground. Not unconscious, I could feel dirt and stone and gravel tearing at my face. Sonyoung seemed to be dragging me by the leg. The grayness darkened and then lightened and darkened again as I struggled to regain full consciousness. When I did, I was aware of a tremendous heaviness around my legs.

I flicked my eyes open and saw Sonyoung standing over me a few paces away, Wilhelmina in his hand. Then I saw that I was lying half-under the curved hull of one of the freighters. Directly above me, high above, a heavy wooden scaffold hung alongside the vessel at the deckline. I glanced down at my legs and saw why I felt such pressure on them. He had placed a heavy metal sheet over the lower half of my body, the kind used for interior bulkhead repairs.

"I could just put a bullet into you, Carter," he said, looking down at me.

"But that could bring others running and I want to leave as quietly as possible. This way, I'll merely loosen the scaffold ropes, and it will plummet down."

He didn't have to diagram it any further. The metal plate would keep me immobile while he used both hands to loosen the scaffold. It would fall and I'd be crushed to death. The upper part of my body was free and my arms movable. Hugo still nestled in the leather sheath up my sleeve. But to throw the stiletto from that position was virtually impossible. But maybe I could drop the blade into my arm and throw it fast and accurately enough to get him before he got me.

"You can't win, Sonyoung," I said, stalling for time. My calm assurance jarred him and he frowned. Then the controlled, slow smile spread across his face again.

"I have won, Carter," he said. "You stopped the actual assassination of your President, but that is relatively unimportant. It took place, to all intents and purposes. Those who have been watching my work will know this from the headlines and the news bulletins. They will know how far my work in mind control can reach."

"Who are these people doing the watching?" I asked.

He shrugged. "It hardly matters if you know now," he said. "My own people of the Vietcong, for one. The representatives of the people's government of China, for another. I, Samuel Sonyoung, have successfully demonstrated a new weapon. Just as military men run tests on new battlefield weapons, this has been a test of a new weapon in the battle for men's minds. Programmed assassination is but one aspect of my work. It is the totally programmed mind we aim at, the mind controlled to do whatever it is programmed to do."

"And you are doing it all for some idealistic reason," I said, heavy on the sarcasm, glancing desperately around as Sonyoung went on.

"Not really," he said. "It is a subject which has fascinated me since childhood. The techniques for accomplishing it are my secret. I expect that my services will now command a rather fabulous price, don't you?"

He laughed, a short, smooth sound of self-satisfaction. But maybe, maybe he was laughing a little too soon. Under the hull, inches from my fingertips, I saw something—a square metal object with a nozzle at one end, an acetylene torch left there by a workman who planned to return to it. Sonyoung had to come closer to loosen the scaffold ropes. It was a chance, but a better one than trying to throw Hugo from my supine position.

I waited, watching. Sonyoung didn't put the Luger down. He cradled it in the palm of his hand as he stepped to the rope where it was knotted to a stanchion on the ground. He had to take his eyes off me as he loosened the rope. I twisted, closed my hand around the handle of the torch and swung it over, pressing once, twice on the starting trigger.

Sonyoung glanced at me, saw the torch, started to pull away—but it was too late. The white-hot flame shot out, hitting his gun hand. He screamed in pain, and the Luger fell to the ground. As he staggered back against the stanchion, he half-turned, holding his seared hand against his body. He was out of range of the torch now. I set it down, managed to raise the sheet of steel just enough for me to wriggle free and drew my legs out from under it.

They were slightly numb from the weight, and I had to pause on hands and knees for a moment to let the circulation come back. Sonyoung turned, his face a mask of cold fury. He aimed a kick at me, not an ordinary kick but the kind delivered by someone who has learned to use his feet the way a boxer uses his hands. I turned aside and took the blow on the side of the head. It sent me sprawling, nonetheless.

Sonyoung dived for the Luger and fired at me, point-blank. But the gun was silent, and he glanced down at it in disgust. The flame from the torch had, in that brief, white-hot instant, welded the firing mechanism shut. He threw the gun at me and ran.

He was racing around the other side of the hull. Enough feeling had returned to my legs now, and I decided to go around the other end and meet him. I got to the bow end of the ship just when he did. I dived for him, and as he whirled around, I saw that he'd picked up a long-handled heavy Stillson wrench.

It was too late to stop my dive, but I twisted my body, hunching up one shoulder, as he brought the heavy wrench down in a short, chopping arc. Excruciating pain exploded in my shoulder, and my left arm suddenly went numb. I landed at his feet, spun around and brought my legs up between his and pulled. He went over backwards, still hanging onto the wrench. Perhaps he was able to work his own mind control techniques on himself because his blistered, bleeding hand didn't seem to handicap him at all.

Hugo was in my hand, and I struck out with the stiletto, plunging it into his arm as he tried to bring up the wrench. He gasped in pain and the heavy wrench fell from his hand. I pulled the stiletto out of his arm, thrust forward with it. He got his hand up in time to keep the blade from plunging into his belly.

The forward motion of my thrust, delivered with full force, brought me off balance. Hugo stabbed into his palm clear out the back of his hand. Sonyoung brought his knee up and, pushing and twisting at the same time, sent me tumbling off to the side. I lost my grip on the stiletto, and as I spun around, I saw Sonyoung yank the blade out of his hand. He leaped at me with it, slashing at me. I dodged the whistling blade and scrambled to my feet. He circled me, Hugo in his injured hand, and I saw pain in his face, mixed with the fury and hate. As I'd suspected that first time I saw him across the room of his apartment, Sonyoung knew judo and karate. His movements were fast and controlled.

I moved back, darting to the right
and then the left to match his feints
and thrusts. Suddenly he lunged, and
I had to leap backwards. My feet hit
something and I went over on my
back. The something I'd hit were a
half-dozen open paint cans. On my
knees beside them, I looked up to see
Sonyoung coming after me, the gleam
of victory in his small button eyes.

I grabbed one of the paint cans and
flung the contents into his face. He
gagged as the thick, black ship's paint
ran down his face. He pawed at his
eyes, looking like some creature out of
a science-fiction movie. I slammed a
hard right into his stomach and he
went backwards, doubled over. I
tossed a right hook, putting everything
I had into it. It caught him flush on
the jaw, and he catapulted backwards.
His body spun around from the force
of the blow and he slammed into the
bow of the ship. He slid down to the
ground, staggered to his feet and
started to run again.

Sonyoung was fighting now on the

strength of desperation and self-pres-
ervation. I went after him, saw him
running blindly, half-staggering, dab-
bing at his eyes, guiding himself by
one hand along the side of the ship. I
caught up to him as he reached the
stern, spun him around and lifted him
off the ground with a tremendous
roundhouse right.

His body flew backwards through
the air, turned in midair and came
down onto the propellor of the ship. He
hung there grotesquely for a moment,
then fell to the ground. I went over to
him. He was dead, his neck broken
when he slammed into the sharp edge
of the propeller.

I stood there for a long moment and
took a deep, deep breath. The world
didn't know it, but mankind had won
a last minute reprieve. How long the
reprieve would last I didn't know.
There would be other Sonyoungs,
fascinated with the prospect of controlling other men's minds. Maybe, by
then, we would have learned the real
value of the independent mind. May-

be, by then, we would have learned how to live with one another. I didn't know. All I knew was that the terrible, dark techniques one man had developed had died with him, and the world would be a better place for it.

I walked out of the shipyard through a side exit, opening the gate from the inside. I wanted to go home and take a nice, cleansing bath.

Hawk called me later that day. The loose ends were being tied together without problems. Ferris Dickson, Hawk had learned, really had been having career problems and a tenuous relationship with the senator. Senator Atkins was in seclusion with his family, under a kind of house arrest.

"The man is completely shattered, of course, Nick," Hawk told me. "The whole thing is one damned messy business. He murdered two people, but is he really a murderer? He was acting under the influence of someone else. It wasn't really Atkins doing the killing. Legally, he might be judged temporarily insane. But there's a tremendous public clamor starting for punishment of course."

It *was* a mess, unquestionably. I hung up, changed and drove across town. Judy Howell answered the door at my knock. She had on a white sweater and a plaid skirt, and she looked like all the cleanliness and freshness there was in the world.

"I've been expecting you," she said, her dark eyes searching mine.

"I've got your exclusive for you," I told her. "Fix me a drink while I give it to you. Do you want to take notes?"

"I'll just listen," she said. "That will be enough."

As we had our drinks, I told her the whole story. She was serious, unsmiling when I'd finished.

"I'll use it," she said: "Most of it, anyway. But I don't really want to use it. There's something chilling about it. I've been sitting here all day thinking about the senator. What a tragedy! What an absolutely stinking, rotten thing."

She put her drink down and came

over to me. "I want to forget, for a little while at least, Nick," she said. "I have an exclusive for you."

Her arms were around my neck and her lips sweet against mine. Her tongue was a moving, thrusting, probing thing with a life of its own. She took my hand and pulled it under her sweater against her straining breast.

"Oh, God, Nick ... make love to me, make love to me," she murmured. I kept my hand against the warm softness of her breast as I looked down at her.

"Why now?" I asked. "Why did you pull away from me before? Why am I one of the 'special people' now?"

"Because I knew you suspected me of something," she said. "I didn't know what, but I felt it. I wouldn't have known if making love wasn't just another way to get to me, to draw me out."

"I still suspect you," I said.

She frowned and drew away, her eyes sparking instantly in that way I'd come to know. "Of what?" she snapped.

"I suspect you of being one helluva passionate woman," I said. I grinned at her.

Her lips parted and she threw herself against me. She raised her sweater, unsnapped her bra and thrust her eager breasts into my hands. I caressed their warmth, their smoothness, and she murmured unintelligibly and closed her eyes.

I picked her up and carried her into the bedroom. Naked, she was magnificent, her figure full and round and firm. My tongue traced soft patterns around the tips of her breasts, and the pink buds rose up in joyful desire. Her hands found me and she cried out in ecstasy. Judy had waited and all the while she had wanted, and the wanting burst forth like a bell ringing in the sunshine. She made love to me with a happy abandon, with an almost childlike pleasure of discovery, running her hands over my body, her lips. She was an eager explorer, reveling in her discoveries, letting pure sensuous pleasure rule her.

When I moved onto her, she cried

out in sheer joy, hugging me with strong, young arms, asking for more and whispering words that were more sound than anything else. Finally, a great gasp rose up from inside her and she quivered, her whole body shaking.

"Nick, Nick," she breathed as I lay beside her. "Stay the night here with me."

"I was counting on it," I said. "And you know something else? My suspicions were right."

She smiled, a wise, very female kind of smile, and her hands reached out for me again. We went to sleep holding each other. Sometime in that night, I felt her stir. I woke to see her moving over onto me, sliding her body over mine. She moved up so that her breasts pressed down onto my face. As I found their sweet lips with my lips she shuddered, and we made love in the dark hours of the morning, slowly and pleasurefully, savoring every moment and every act. Dawn stroked the window pane as we dropped off to sleep again.

The doorbell woke us. Judy tossed a robe on, the salmon terry cloth one I'd seen before, and went to the door. It was a special messenger with a letter, and she brought it into me, eyes wide with apprehension.

"It's from the senator," she said, a quiver in her voice. "I know his handwriting. Spending every day with him on that series I was doing, we got to know each other very well. I . . . I became very fond of him and he said often how much he liked my being around. I guess we developed a kind of a father-daughter relationship almost."

"And now he's written you?" I said. "That's not surprising then."

"You read it, Nick," she said. "I'm afraid. I've a funny feeling what it might say."

I opened the letter and looked at the large, well-formed script.

"My dearest Judy," I read aloud. "We have had so many lovely talks on so many topics that I have come to know you as the understanding person you are. Therefore, I do not need to tell you what I am going through now. Indeed, I doubt that I could. I have assassinated two fine men, two of my friends and colleagues. I almost assassinated our President. Lawyers tell me I have a defense, one that could probably set me free of these terrible charges. But no defense can set me free of myself, of what I feel, of the guilt and anguish that is inside me.

"No, my dear, I have decided that no matter what the lawyers do to set me free of the technical charges, I can never be free again. And one additional haunting thought lives with me now. I will never know what other dark deeds have been implanted in my mind, impulses which could be released perhaps at some future date. No matter how much they tried, neither my family nor my friends could ever look upon me in the same way again. More importantly, I can never face myself again. There aren't any words to wipe away what I feel. There aren't men wise enough to give me a philosophy of living again.

"And so, Judy, I write this to you so you may tell the world, as you see fit, what I have said. I will be on my last journey when you read this, my dear. May God have mercy on my soul. Your friend, Herbert Atkins."

Judy was sobbing before I was half-way through the letter. Now she came to me, her body shaking with wracking, gasping sobs. I shook her by the shoulders.

"Stop it," I said sharply. "Maybe there's still time. He writes about his 'last journey'. Where would he be going? Think, Judy. You and he talked about so many things. Is there some particular favorite spot of his?"

"Yes . . . oh, yes," she said, eyes opening wide. "He used to tell me about a high bluff in the Catoctin Mountains where he'd go to sit and think whenever he had a particularly tricky problem to work out."

"Get your clothes on," I said, grabbing my shirt. "We'll give it all we can."

The Catoctin Mountains is a small range northwest of Washington in Loudon County Virginia. We got into the car and I took off, making believe it was an airplane. Judy described the bluff as best she could from what the senator had told her and we were lucky. We found the road leading to it without any trouble, probably because it was the first steep road leading off the main highway.

The car raced up the mountainside and then, as we negotiated a sharp curve, I saw the senator's car with the official emblem on the rear pulled over on the road. Another sharp curve lay just ahead. The side of the road was a sheer drop.

"You stay here," I said, getting out of the car. I ran around the curve. Senator Atkins was standing at the edge of the bluff, looking toward me; he must have heard the car when we drove up. Now he raised one hand in a salute and stepped out into space. I stood still for a moment, then turned and walked back to the car. Judy read what had happened in my face. She gave a little anguished cry.

"Let's go home," I said, as she came into my arms, resting her head on my shoulder. "You've got a story to tell the American people, with a message from a Senator of the United States."

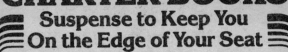

CHARTER BOOKS
Suspense to Keep You
On the Edge of Your Seat

DECEIT AND DEADLY LIES
by Franklin Bandy   06517-1   **$2.25**

MacInnes and his Psychological Stress Evaluator could tell when anyone was lying, but could he discover the lies he was telling to himself?

VITAL STATISTICS by Thomas Chastain 86530-5 **$1.95**

A missing body, several murders and a fortune in diamonds lead J. T. Spanner through a mystery in which New York itself may be one of the suspects. By the author of *Pandora's Box* and *9-1-1*.

THE KREMLIN CONSPIRACY
by Sean Flannery   45500-X   **$2.25**

Detente espionage set in Moscow as two top agents find themselves as pawns in a game being played against the backdrop of a Presidential visit to the Kremlin.

THE BLACKSTOCK AFFAIR
by Franklin Bandy   06650   **$2.50**

A small town, a deadly medical mystery, and the corruption of power provide the dangerous mix in this new KEVIN MACINNES thriller.

SIGMET ACTIVE by Thomas Page 76330-8 **$2.25**

The author of the bestselling HESPHAESTUS PLAGUE presents another thriller proving it isn't nice to fool Mother Nature.

Available wherever paperbacks are sold or use this coupon

 ACE CHARTER BOOKS
P.O. Box 400, Kirkwood, N.Y. 13795

Please send me the titles checked above. I enclose _____.
Include 75¢ for postage and handling if one book is ordered; 50¢ per book for two to five. If six or more are ordered, postage is free. California, Illinois, New York and Tennessee residents please add sales tax.

NAME_____

ADDRESS_____

CITY_____ STATE_____ ZIP_____

Xa

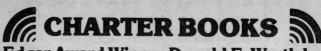